Artifacts of Fae

Artifacts of Fae

Lucia Jex-Blake

{ 1 }

CHAPTER ONE:

A spell had set Geena's jacket on fire so she was forced to tear it off as the flames licked around her.

I liked that damn thing, Geena thought as she threw it down and dodged another spell.

It almost looked like a swarm of multicolored fireflies were following Geena, but the reality was that they were violent spells being cast in hopes of stopping her. Between her panting and the sound of breaking leaves and twigs, she could only hear a slight hum of the spell before it was right on top of her. If she hadn't been running away from them so long, she wouldn't have gotten so good at this. Running, dodging, and surviving.

Turning slightly, she ran for a narrow opening within the tall trees, hoping that going deeper into the woods would deter her pursuers. Clutching her wand, she aimed the best she could for the farther end of the opening. Either luck or skill let her successfully cast a spell that set the shrubbery on fire. She leapt over the small flames before helping them grow into a wall to separate her from them. She was unaware of the pair of eyes watching her as her auburn hair glowed with her magic. The person watching Geena could've sworn it almost looked like... but it's impossible.

With a wall of flames in front of her, Geena turned to assess her surroundings but only heard a faint flutter of wings before she saw a figure drop from above and land softly in front of her.

She had her wand up and steady. "Who are you?"

"Someone who can help you," the soft voice spoke surely as they approached Geena.

"How do I know I can trust you?"

"I'd rather you not burn our forest to the ground, and you need help."

Geena's wand dropped a few inches, thinking through her options, before sticking it in the holster on her forearm and redoing her hair to get the free tendrils from her face.

She nodded and said, "Okay, what do we need to do?"

"First we'll get a bit of a head start, then I need you to put out the fire." The girl flew inches above the ground over to Geena.

"You're a Faerie, why would you help me?" Geena blurted out as she crossed the remaining distance between them.

"You're not like the rest of them, or else they wouldn't be trying to kill you," the faerie girl spoke as Geena finished gathering her things and put them in the bag that had fallen out of. "Plus I'm in a good mood tonight." She finished with a shrug.

The angered voices on the other side were getting louder and that meant they were getting closer.

Snapping back to attention, the faerie said, "Follow me after you put out the fire, as we get closer I'll need to be touching you for you to be able to get in."

"Get in where?" Geena asked.

"Questions later. We need to go now." The girl's wings started up and the thrumming could've calmed Geena to sleep if the adrenaline in her body didn't make her want to fight a pack of wolves.

The faerie girl flew and Geena ran and after some distance was put between them and the fire, Geena cast a spell that looked like a huge wave to wash down the flames and knock down the horde of wizards on the other side of it.

"Nice job," the faerie girl spoke, not even out of breath a little as Geena was barely keeping up with the flying girl. Unexpectedly, spells started exploding around from the right.

"Hurry!" The faerie girl rushed, as Geena began to cast a series of protection spells.

Ahead, Geena saw an almost perfect line of trees, and as they got closer, the center tree began to open up and glow. Rays of light escaped from the opening, and it would've been beautiful if Geena wasn't so focused on not dying.

"Almost there, come closer to me," The faerie yelled, but Geena could only focus on the opening.

With an extra burst of energy, she cast a spell that blasted the closest wizards away before she sprinted into the opening of the trees, forgetting she needed the faerie's touch to enter.

The light was blinding as she went through, but it enveloped her in warmth. Geena took a minute to adjust her eyes as she sat on the ground with her head in her hands before the faerie girl knelt in front of her.

"You got in by yourself." It was a statement, not a question. "You shouldn't have been able to if you're just a wizard." The faerie girl brushed dirt off of Geena's pants before standing up straight. "I'm Juniper." She held her hand out as her dragonfly-like wings disappeared, folding in on themselves before vanishing into her back.

Geena took her hand and gave the most firm shake she could, but she knew the faerie could feel her hand trembling. "Geena."

"Let's get you settled before I take you to the Council. You look like shit and in need of a nap," Juniper said with a laugh before turning and walking down a trail that led to a leafy area with big and small huts scattered between the trees and plants. Geena took a deep breath before she stood up and followed.

———

Potent was the only word Geena could think of to describe everything around her. The colors of the area were fully saturated, Geena had never seen anything so beautiful. This place was overflowing with life. The air felt like a warm hug and smelled fresh, clean, and inviting. She sat on Juniper's cushioned porch swing and studied her surroundings. Geena went to go through her supplies when she realized she threw her other bag off with her jacket in the scuffle.

Sighing, she cursed at herself and began unlacing her boots, trying to figure what exact shade of purple the flowers in front of the porch were, when a swarm of butterflies hummed closer and landed on their petals. She stared in awe.

"Hey." The sudden voice caused Geena to snap up, wand drawn and ready to defend herself. Her hand holding on to her boot was shaking, but her grip on the wand was steady.

"Sorry," said Juniper, putting her hands up in surrender. "Got a few people who will let you crash in their hut tonight." She gestured behind her. "I still have patrols tonight or else you could've stayed with me."

Three people approached from a beaten path that traced around and through the other huts, Geena immediately took note of the wand holsters on their arms. "Wizards." Rather than relax, Geena aimed at the boy in the center of the little group. "Like me."

Laughter bubbled out of Juniper. "Most definitely not like you! These unfortunate bastards can't get in without a Faerie escort..." Juniper drifted off waiting for Geena to come to a conclusion herself.

"So am I a Faerie?" Geena lowered her wand, distracted by her thoughts, and she sank back into the swing.

"Most likely not, considering the wand and the everything else about you," Juniper waved her hand at Geena to encapsulate the 'everything' she mentioned, before she suddenly shook her head like a thought suddenly occurred to her. "When's the last time you ate?"

Geena's laugh was dry. "Maybe two days ago."

Without another word, Juniper smacked one of the wizards and after a few seconds of pouting he went into Juniper's house. Geena looked at Juniper confused.

"He likes to cook," Juniper replied with a shrug. "While he does that, you're going to meet the Council."

"I thought I looked like shit." Geena met Juniper's gaze with a smirk.

"Exactly, maybe they'll take it easy on you," Juniper's retort caused the other two wizards to chuckle. Geena couldn't tell if they were laughing at her appearance, or because the Council didn't 'take it easy' on people, especially wizards who don't need a faerie to get into their land.

———

Five faeries, sitting in thrones that formed a slight semicircle, faced Geena with quizzical brows. The room was wide and Geena could not make sense of where nature ended and man-made, or faerie-made features began. Tons of flowers descended from above and created murals on the walls, or maybe the walls were just flowers. Geena was equally awestruck by her surroundings as she was the beautiful faeries of the Council. Juniper noticed her nerves and put her hand on Geena's shoulder to silently show her some support. The five faeries staring her down may be ethereal in their beauty, but they were on a throne for a reason. Geena could sense the power radiating from them, even as they sat calmly, waiting. Geena gave Juniper a tightlipped smile in response before giving her full attention to the five thrones.

"So you're the wizard that snuck in?" a strong voice called out.

"Sorrel! That is not how we greet a guest." An ethereal faerie stood as she spoke and her platinum hair floated around her as she approached Geena. "I'm Vinca, Queen of Fire, and you must be our new guest." Geena was frozen for a moment before she shook the hand the small figure extended to her. "Ignore Sorrel, he's... well, it doesn't matter."

Geena matched the gentle smile Vinca gave before bowing her head in Sorrel's direction in the center throne, trying to be respectful but not knowing any faerie customs.

"Sorrel, King of Earth," Vinca quickly spoke before gesturing to the next occupied seat, "Cerise, Queen of Air." Geena dipped her head toward the vision of reds and pinks before her brain processed the red hair and pink skin. Vinca continued, "Dula, Queen of Water." Geena looked at the intense sight that was Dula and met molten silver eyes that looked through her. "And our newest royal," Vinca said, ignoring a scoff that came from the thrones, "Orrin, King of Water." The immense faerie king approached Geena. She looked at Juniper worriedly before returning her attention to Orrin, noticing the thick curled horns that protruded from his head, as he stood and stared at her in silence.

"Hi," Geena squeaked out with an awkward wave before shutting her eyes in embarrassment wanting to disintegrate into the floral air. She began wringing her hands, ignoring the dirt that pilled together as she did. Geena only opened her eyes when she realized that the King had taken her hands and was making cool streams of water float over them, ridding them of dirt.

"Hello, Geena." Her eyes met Orrin's in a moment of confusion. She hadn't told the Royals her name, and but Juniper's loud gasp, neither had she.

"How do you..."

"I knew your mother," Orrin interrupted, but before he could explain, he was interrupted himself.

"Knew? Please, the two of you were disgustingly in love," the reddish pink faerie spoke in a rage, her hair expanding. By the time Geena remembered her name and power, the silver eyes looked to Orrin before sending a wave, a literal wave, to force the pink faerie from her throne.

Orrin grinned in acknowledgment to Dula before Vinca, the platinum-haired queen, said, "Cerise, be nice." Vinca turned to Dula and met her silver gaze. "Dula, leave."

Unbothered, Dula approached Geena and shook her hand. "It's nice to finally meet you." Silver wings that resembled a butterflies' stretched out behind Dula before she fluttered away.

"Do you all fly?" Geena usually had a better filter on things she said, but her heart was pounding so loud she could barely hear herself say anything. She only knew she had actually said it out loud when she felt the vibrations of her voice in her throat.

Juniper laughed, "They wish they were all cool enough."

The break in tension caused Vinca to smile at Geena before going over to Cerise to check on her as she gasped for air, leaving Geena with Orrin.

"You know, you almost look just like *her*," Orrin began, his voice trembling. Geena, overwhelmed, couldn't find her voice, so she simply nodded. It wasn't anything new to be told she looked like her mother.

"Food's ready!" a young man yelled as he burst through the door. Geena recognized him as the one Juniper introduced to her earlier, the wizard that likes to cook.

"Well at least something good is happening now," the blue faerie, Sorrel, spoke as he began approaching Geena, but Vinca intercepted him with a shake of her head. "This is bullshit," the faerie complained. He turned to leave and before he exited he shouted back to the cook, "I want a blackberry cobbler tomorrow, *Purse*." The door slammed shut, leaving Geena with Juniper, three Royals, and *'Purse.'*

"Let's get you some food and some clean clothes," Vinca stated, her platinum hair framing her face, as she threaded one of her arms through Geena's and led her to a different exit. Geena turned back to Orrin, whose longing gaze followed her as she left.

CHAPTER TWO:

"Orrin loved your mother very much, practically worshiping the ground she walked on," Vinca said while brushing through Geena's hair as gently as she could, but it was a nest since she didn't have a brush to maintain it while on the run. Vinca took breaks to let Geena eat and because she didn't like hurting her.

"They were so happy together. The rest of us couldn't believe it, a faerie and a wizard, in love and happy," Vinca paused, her eyes clouded as she was lost in a memory. "I'll be honest, I didn't know exactly what love that wasn't platonic looked like until I saw them." Vinca's eyes snapped back to reality. "You look just like her. Juniper told me while we got your food that she thought you were your mom as you were running away from those other wizards."

Vinca bent down behind Geena and met her eyes in the mirror. "Wall of fire was a nice touch, by the way." Vinca's blue eyes flashed like flames before returning to their original hue. Pushing her sleeves up, she continued working knots from Geena's mass of red hair. "From Cerise's reaction, I bet you can gather that not everyone was thrilled about the union. Then again, Cerise somehow manages to not be happy about much."

"Who is Cerise again?" Geena interrupted.

"The pinkish faerie—the Queen of Air," Vinca answered before continuing, "Orrin was distraught one day and said your mom was gone and he'd never see her again. He's been this barely emotive statue since." Vinca's voice was airy and soft, despite the topic.

There was a knock at the door and someone peeked their head in, silver eyes peered into the room before the rest of them followed.

"Dula!" Vinca rushed to hug her. "I was just telling Geena a little about her parents."

"Wait. Parents?" Geena stood, the chair scraping against the floor with the sudden movement.

"Oh shoot, forgot to ease into that one." Vinca deflated and was met with Dula patting down her hair with affection.

"This is why you're a fire faerie, not very subtle." Dula's voice was cold, but not cruel. Geena gathered that Dula just wasn't someone who you turn to for warmth. "Vinnie's right though, Orrin is your father." Ignoring Vinca thumping her for the nickname, Dula replaced Vinca's job in taming Geena's hair. "Told me I could be your godmother should we ever find you, however, I'll let you decide if I'm allowed the honor. Your mom was a good friend to me; I was actually the one to tell her to give Orrin a shot. They fell in love quickly after being friends for so long. When your mom found out about you, she and Orrin decided to split to keep you safe." Dula caught a knot too fast and mumbled an apology. "The only thing they loved more than each other was you, so they played the deadbeat dad card so no wizards would question your mother wherever she was staying and Orrin disappeared from her life."

Dula stopped and rummaged through the drawers of the vanity until she found a magenta cream in a glass container that had *Detangler* written on it. "Who made this?" Dula turned to Vinca, who responded with a shrug.

"Can you go to our hut and get mine? Can't afford for this unruly mess to continue," Vinca giggled and practically skipped out of the room.

––––––

Geena could've cried from the warm feeling of being clean, fed, and in new clothes that weren't her size but close enough. However, no matter how grateful she was to the Council, Juniper, and the other wizards who she hadn't had many encounters with, she refused to let her guard down completely. They could all be lying about her mom and her "dad." She got a new bag and stocked it with food they'd given her and what little she had before encountering them. She kept her holster on her arm and her wand ready to cast any protective spells any minute. When she was around them, it was harder to keep her guard up, she so badly wanted to stay here and be safe. So the moments she had to herself, she made up for it by ensuring she could depart any second if necessary.

She was currently in a room that would be "hers" for the time being. Surrounded in neutral colors, she relaxed as much as she could and rubbed her sore muscles in her calves as she digested everything they told her.

Could my mom have been with him? Could he be my dad? She never talked about him. She never talked about anything before me. She was my mom and my teacher. Taught me magic herself. Spells, charms, and what little potions she knew. Preparing me for something, preparing me for...

There was a knock at the door.

"Come in." Geena's voice was raspy and fading, she hadn't done so much talking in a long time. Being alone and on the run from some rabid wizards with no idea what they wanted from her caused her to live a more solitary life.

"I brought you some soup." Vinca entered with a tray that carried a steaming bowl and a glass of water. "Figured you needed something simple until you get used to eating regularly."

Geena took the tray and offered her thanks. "You all have done a lot for me in such a short time, even though I'm standoffish, I am extremely grateful."

Vinca's smile was bright and stretched until Geena couldn't see her eyes anymore, radiating warmth. "I also have something else for you," Vinca said, sitting on the foot of the bed and smoothing out the bottom of her dress that almost matched the color of her hair, she set down a stack of paper and some pictures. "Those are photos and letters from Orrin. He said if you were anything like your mother you would need a little more proof to trust us." She added jazz hands around the stack as she said *proof*.

"Thank you, Vinca. Or—uh—Queen Vinca?"

Giggling slightly, she replied, "Vinca is just fine, we faeries aren't very strict on titles in most informal situations. We're very kind and accepting, you know?" She winked and stood up before making her way to the door, "If you need anything, light the candle on your bedside table and either me or Dula will head over here from our hut."

"Wait—what about Orrin? Will I get to talk to him?"

"He wanted you to have those before the two of you talked, that way maybe some questions can be skipped over and you can ask others." Vinca recited monotonously, obviously repeating another's words before she returned to her airy and mystical voice, "Personally, I think Orrin just needs time himself. He never thought he'd get to meet you and with you being alone, we've guessed that sweet Mia isn't with us anymore."

"She told me before she died that she'd always be with me and those she loved. She said I could always find her where there was water." Geena's throat began to close with her grief. "I always assumed that was because of the reflection, and I look like her. It's because of him though, isn't it?"

Vinca deflated at Geena's revelation, knowing where she was going, she finished for her, "King of Water. He actually taught her how to swim, you know? She used to just flop around and somehow manage to float." Vinca figured maybe offering a sweet memory would ease the sting of learning her mother's past.

"I think I'd like to be alone now, if that's alright."

"Goodnight, Geena," Opening the door, Vinca added one thing before leaving: "You are safe here, regardless of anything else, I will take care of you."

Geena offered a sad smile, ignoring the tears collecting in her eyes, and watched the door shut leaving her with a darkening room as the sun surrendered to night.

Geena surrendered soon after, dreaming of oceans and her mother's voice reminding her that *water is beautiful, and it gives life as much as it takes.*

{ 3 }

CHAPTER THREE:

No one interrupted Geena until the afternoon, leaving her the morning to read the letters and study the photos Vinca left her the previous night. The letters were years worth of writing between her mom and Orrin. Geena basically read a story of the two of them going from friends to being in love. From meeting each other when Orrin saved her mom from drowning to saying when Geena was born. The second she saw her mother's handwriting, all doubts dissolved and Geena succumbed to the tears that had threatened since her conversation with Vinca. She ran her fingers along the dried ink that flowed with her mother's elegant script. A memory clouded her for a moment, her mother's hand around her own, guiding her chubby toddler hands to write words. Unable to face the unfamiliar horde of people that Geena knew was waiting outside her four walls, she picked up the box of matches, lit the candle, and waited for Vinca or Dula.

After a few minutes there was a knock at the door.

"Hello gorgeous. Let's eat then wanna go swimming?" Dula closed the door behind her with her foot and carried a tray full of food towards Geena. She found it hard to feel awkward with Dula. Whatever stilted atmosphere should have existed, Dula cut through it and strutted in comfort, leading the way for Geena to follow. While Dula was distributing the food between them, Geena was able to study her in a way she hadn't before. Dula was all sharp features, from her blunt black hair cut below her chin to her perfectly manicured nails. There was not a single thing out of place, all precise and tended to.

"You're staring," Dula spoke without looking up, continuing to drizzle honey over her bowl of fruit.

"You are very pretty." She paused, clearing her throat, then admitted, "Your beauty is intimidating." Geena took her own bowl and began eating all of the blueberries first.

"Good." Dula looked pleased with Geena's observation. "Thank you."

"Any questions on that matter?" Dula gestured to the stack of letters and photos on the bedside table.

"I don't know. It seems so hard to believe. My mom never talked about her life before me." Geena sighed, ate the last blueberry and started eating the blackberries next. "I'm happy to know that she was loved but I wonder what would've happened if I didn't—"

Dula met Geena with a sharp look that silenced her. "You won't find any answers to that. No use wasting your energy trying to flesh it out." Dula's nails clicked around her glass as she picked it up and took a sip. "What's done is done."

"Did he really save her from drowning? Like is all the stuff in the letters real?" Geena asked.

"He did. It's all real; Orrin wouldn't have kept any letters if they were fake."

The rest of their breakfast was in silence but neither of them felt uncomfortable. Dula was looking over the photos while Geena finished her fruit bowl and watched Dula react to the photos.

"I have some pictures of me and your mom if you want more to look at." Geena met silver eyes that for the first time looked something other than confident and bold; Dula's eyes were sad.

"She may have been Orrin's love, but she was my friend first. She saved my life, in more ways than one." Dula put down a picture of her mom shoving cake into Orrin's face with a sad smile.

"She saved your life?"

"Oh yeah. I was newest to the Kings and Queens at the time. Most fae weren't comfortable with me yet, so I was alone a lot and I got into a bad headspace. Your mom was the first person to see my beauty and strength and not fear it but admire it. Orrin only joined after Mia left when an old faerie king wanted to step back and spend more time with his family." Dula answered.

"How does he still look the same?" Geena inquired.

"The same way you wave a stick and shit happens." Dula's sensitive moment was gone. "Magic. We age slower with our magic. The only magic we have in common with wizards is making potions. Faerie potions take longer to make, and I assume the process is a little different, but they are more potent and work better."

"Speaking of potions, what's the one that you used on my hair?" Geena's tone switched to a lighter, excited one and began running her fingers through her hair, something she hadn't been able to do in months without catching knots.

"Forget swimming, we'll do faerie potions 101 today." Dula stood, slipped her heels back on and went to the door to call out "Hey Juni! Do you mind taking this stuff back to *Purse* in the kitchen?"

Geena heard a distant muffled "Fine."

"Purse?" Geena asked, looking at Dula for answers.

"Percy. Perc. I'm sure you'll meet him soon enough."

Tying up her hair, Geena finished by sticking her wand through it and walked out of her room to what Juniper called "Dula's evil lab".

————

After spending the whole afternoon with Dula learning about how faerie potions worked, Geena was fascinated. Faerie potions had to be made under certain temperatures and adding ingredients at specific times. Geena was used to making wizard potions that, for the most part, you could make by adding ingredients in any order and usually only altering the temperature once or twice. After all of the new information, Geena was exhausted. Especially when Dula wanted to see if Geena herself could start a faerie potion, which she managed but struggled to do so.

"Doesn't help Orrin is shit with potions," was all Dula said in response.

Tiredly walking back to the "wizard hut" as it was dubbed by the faeries, Geena reexamined the scenery around her, having not seen the beauty of it at night. Soft lights emitted from each hut, Geena could feel the warmth radiate from them. The stars were the brightest she had ever seen, nothing polluting her view of them.

Geena wandered over to a small pond and sat by it, watching fireflies twinkling across the water. Breathing in the calming air, she processed all she had stumbled upon since running into Juniper. She still had the wizard mafia, or whatever they were, after her, as they had been for years. Geena never knew why, and surely didn't stick around to find out either. Now, she had faeries as acquaintances, protectors, and strangest of all, family.

Looking down at the water Geena studied her reflection, wondering if her mom ever looked at her own in this pond too.

"What am I supposed to do, Mama?" Geena watched her lips in her reflection. Wishing she could just dissolve into the water and never deal with her chaotic life again.

Even though she knew it wouldn't actually go to her mother, Geena picked a small orange flower from where she was sitting. She ran her fingers over the soft petals for a minute. Wishing that she would be strong enough to make it through this, she put the flower in her pond, and told her mother goodbye.

————

She felt the hum of magic in the air before she heard the screaming. Geena woke up and was out of her room ready to run before she remembered where she was, that she was with faeries that would protect her. She had her wand pointed at the individuals in the kitchen that were the source of the screaming and the buzz of magic resonating in the air. Geena could feel her own auburn hair sparking with her magic, ready for her to use. It looked like a bomb went off in the kitchen, white powder covered most of the floor around one of the girls who turned to the boy and let him know what she thought of it.

"You absolute shit-head! It'll take me forever to get this out of my hair, Perseus!" The boy was laughing, Perseus, Geena recognized him as the wizard that likes to cook. The screaming girl and the other girl at the table were familiar but still foreign to Geena. Hoping to avoid interaction, Geena went to go back to her room before she was called after, but as she began to back away a voice was directed towards her.

"Hey! She's alive," the boy made his way to Geena, disregarding her raised wand. "Meda, Mirzam, the two of you are being extremely rude by not introducing yourself to this fine beautiful creature."

One of the women smacked him on the back of his head. Powder settled across the kitchen as the girl with the powder matted in her hair approached Geena, hand extended. Geena lowered her wand and took her hand.

"I'm Andromeda, but you can just call me Meda." Meda, regardless of her current state, was a picture of a goddess. Long, curly hair that draped down her shoulders to cease at her waist. She was tall and moved like a ballerina, practically floating through the air.

"Geena," she said, shaking her hand. "Nice to meet you, Meda."

The other girl approached Geena, significantly shorter compared to Meda and Perseus whose height was almost identical, towering over the two of them. This girl's skin was a rich dark color where Meda and Perseus were golden. Her hair was tightly put up, where Geena would have flyaways, hers were neatly laid down, framing her face. Her fingers were covered in ink as she had been fervently writing before the interruption, but Geena didn't hesitate to shake her hand.

"I'm Mirzam, but I'll answer to almost everything. Percy here has a tendency to call me anything except my name."

"To complete the trio, I'm Perseus, or Percy, or Perc, or your future husband," Percy said as he bowed, kissing the back of Geena's hand and holding eye contact with her, not flinching when Meda smacked his head again. Too stunned to even begin to feel awkward or flustered, Geena stood like a statue until Percy released her hand, letting it fall to her side.

"Ignore my twin brother," Meda said. "He thinks he's hot shit."

"Well, he is one of those," Mirzam interjected.

Percy said "hot" at the same time Meda said "shit."

Mirzam met Geena's gaze and shrugged. "Siblings."

"Twins!" The duo corrected.

"Anyway, would you like some pancakes, gorgeous?" Percy inquired, wiggling his eyebrows at her.

"Only if they are blueberry pancakes with a side of blackberries," Geena replied with a voice full of sarcasm as she wanted to release some of the tension from her body. She expected the request to be ignored and was ready to take a normal pancake, but when she moved to go do so, her hand was lightly slapped away.

"Does that look like a blueberry pancake?" Percy gave her a stern glare before escorting her to the table, pulling out a chair for Geena to sit. "I'll bring it to you when I have finished." His smile was soft, the arrogance of earlier had faded a little, but only a little.

Geena looked at the two girls who were engrossed in a conversation related to training for something. After a few minutes, a plate was placed in front of her next to a small bowl.

"Blueberry pancakes and blackberries on the side for the lovely lady, as requested," Percy announced with a wink.

Not even her exhaustion from waking sooner than she'd like because of the morning's events could stop the blush that made a home of her face.

{ **4** }

CHAPTER FOUR:

The quiet morning was interrupted when Juniper burst into the wizard hut as the four were eating breakfast.

"Training resumes today bitches!" Juniper bellowed, punching her fist in the air when she was met with Percy's groan.

"I think I am needed more in the kitchens than I will ever be in the battlefield," Percy said with the best puppy-dog face he could manage.

As Juniper was laughing at his whining, Geena cut in, "Training for battle? I thought faeries were peaceful?"

"They are, but they are not weak. Faeries find it very important to obtain a balanced community," Mirzam explained, not looking up from her book. "Everyone knows the basics in healing, fighting, and all that good stuff."

"Wouldn't you just want the best to be utilizing their talents all the time?" Geena questioned.

"Nope," Juniper said as she stole a piece of bacon from Meda's plate, "what if something happens to them? Who takes over if the rest of us are clueless? We build each other as a community and push each other to become better. That's why we train!" Juniper stood, doing her best to make a superhero pose that caused the rest of them to giggle at her antics.

"We've been training since we got here," Meda told Geena. "We go on some missions for the faeries when it is harder for them to do it themselves. It's how we pay our rent, I guess."

"Am I joining?" Geena asked.

"Sweetheart," Percy said as he took Geena's hand, "You're the reason we got a break." He quickly planted another kiss on the back of her hand and barely dodged the slap Andromeda meant to give him.

"Gotta be faster than that, Meda!" Percy ran out of the kitchen before she could try to smack him again.

The girls laughed as Meda huffed in annoyance, angrily biting into her last piece of bacon.

———

The training hall was the second biggest room Geena had seen since she'd been staying with the faeries. The Council room being the biggest. Instead of the floral décor of the Council room, the training hall was all lethal business. Any wall that wasn't covered in weapons was a target. Somehow it was still beautiful to Geena, as she walked next to a wall of swords and knives when one caught her eye. She ran a finger along the handle of a sword and noticed that at the base of the blade, it was covered in thorns.

The thorns began to move, wrapping themselves around Geena's hand, and before she could pull it away, they tightened. Geena winced as they broke through her skin.

"Do not touch things that are not yours." The other faerie King approached Geena, she scrambled her brain to put a name to the king with iridescent blue hair and pointed ears. "I am talking to you, half-breed. Did you not get any of your father's wit?" *What was his name?* King of earth.

"Sorrel!" Vinca called out, burning up the thorns that had slowly been cutting further into Geena's hand. The flames warmly surrounded her hand, burning up the thorns but only tickling her skin. Vinca was an image of fury, as she got closer to the two of them, Geena struggled to breathe from the heat radiating from the faerie queen. Her usual platinum hair was almost a blue fire as she stared down at Sorrel.

"Be nice, or I will scorch you." Vinca's voice was like welded metal, hot and unforgiving. "Remember last time?" Sorrel backed away with his hands up, looking almost regretful. He didn't say anything as he turned to leave.

"Are you okay, honey?" Vinca was back to her normal joyful self, like flipping a switch.

"Y-yeah, just shocked me, that's all." Geena was surprised that despite Vinca's small stature, she made quite the towering scary figure when necessary.

Vinca turned to search for Sorrel again, then sent a ball of fire to hit his backside.

Sorrel yelped, "Vinca, my ass!"

Vinca simply gave him a wink and giggled with Geena as they realized the fire had burned through all of the clothing on his butt.

"Mortimer," Vinca called to a nearby faerie, "do you mind getting some healing salve for these cuts?"

"Of course, Queen Vinca." The boy nodded his head of shaggy brown hair and retreated quickly.

"Sorrel will be back, we should get a drink and wait until he's ready for us again." Vinca told the group.

———

The training hall was decorated like a forest. The wizards, other than Geena, looked at each other, confused as this was an anomaly compared to the normal training sessions they had been to.

"Today, we will be doing a demo fight." Sorrel announced from a branch of a tree closest to the entrance. He used his power to lower the branch and himself to the ground before returning the branch to its original position. "First, we will do teams, then we will do one on one attacks. Powers and spells are allowed. The only rule is nothing fatal."

Meda looked unfazed by the announcement of training differently. She simply made sure that her hair was secure in the braid she chose for today. Mirzam was studying the layout of the faux forest, planning where to attack from or hide. Percy was jittery, bouncing from one foot to the other, and only stopped when Geena put a hand on his shoulder.

Sorrel was studying Geena, noticing that she wasn't prepping herself or planning anything the way the wizards seemed to once he announced the training for the day. She was eerily calm, like a pond in the morning before anything caused a ripple.

"Team A is Meda, Mirzam, and myself." Sorrel announced. "Team B is Percy, Geena, and our special guest Vinca."

Percy and Geena went over to Vinca to start planning a basic idea for offense and defense.

As the fight was about to start, Geena could feel the magic concentrate in the room. She knew that spells would be hurled through the air like they were when she was being chased by The Score. It was like an explosion went off as the fight began. The trees were alive, swinging their branches and using their roots to make it hard to balance on the ground. If any branches got close enough, they were quickly turned to ash that floated in the air, making it hard to see and breathe. Geena ran over to Percy, who was maintaining a shield spell to keep Meda and Mirzam's attacks from endangering anyone while they combated the murderous trees. She quickly cast a spell that would make it easier for the two of them to see and breathe regardless of the ash and debris flying around.

That's when Geena felt it. Her magic had always tried to warn her of danger, and she never hesitated to listen. She grabbed Percy's hand and started running toward Vinca on the other side of the room. When the duo had made it about halfway, an explosion erupted from behind them, knocking them down. The floor was shaking like something was beating on it repeatedly.

"Get up, Percy! We have to keep moving." Geena looked at his face when she spoke and could see that his eyes were unfocused. Regardless of this being a demo fight, Geena recognized what was happening with him. It had happened with her mom a number of times when an attack had gotten too close for comfort. He was shutting down.

She slung his arm around her shoulder and continued walking toward Vinca. Her flames were suffocating and almost solid blue in their color. Percy was on autopilot as Geena guided them behind a wall of flames, where they found Vinca standing still; the only tense part of her body was her clenched fists.

"Vinca, he's out." Geena said.

"What happened?" Her voice was calm in the juxtaposition of all the chaos around them.

"You know how people have a fight or flight response?"

Vinca nodded at Geena.

"This is the third option, freeze."

Vinca called a firebird and sent a message over to Sorrel, calling the fight off. Immediately, the flames disappeared, and the trees returned to their original positions. Geena stood in front of Percy, casting cooling spells around them to help with the heat radiating around them. She was starting to wash some dirt from his hand when Meda all but pushed Geena out of the way to get in front of her brother.

"Mirzam," Meda said, "go get the calming syrup from our hut."

"What's going on?" Sorrel asked as he leisurely made his way over.

"He's panicking. I have to calm him down before he completely freaks out."

It took almost an hour to calm Percy down fully. Sorrel dismissed them for lunch and told them to come back after for one on one demo fights. Percy was told to either stay at the wizard hut, or he could watch the others finish training but could not participate anymore for the day. When he decided to watch, Meda refused to leave his side in case he started to panic again. Which left Mirzam and Geena to go against each other in a fight. The same rules applied as the team fight, but no one could help either of the girls.

"The fight stops when someone is injured or is unconscious." Sorrel told them.

"Or if one of you has said you've had enough," Vinca added, looping her arms around one of Sorrel's.

"Yeah, that too" He rolled his eyes, "but I'd prefer to see the fight play out."

———

Mirzam warned Geena that she had a new invention she wanted to try but said nothing else as the two opponents went to their starting positions. Geena felt her magic tingling under her skin, ready to move her body if Geena hesitated. Sorrel was counting down when her magic warned her to get low immediately. Geena never really understood how she so clearly understood her magic, but it was always right, so she always listened.

"3, 2," Sorrel paused, enjoying the anticipation. "1."

Geena went down immediately and missed a huge spell from Mirzam as it screamed over her. Geena could see Mirzam thinking, calculating, and planning. She was distracted by all of the possibilities that she didn't react when Geena threw a spell at her that knocked her down.

"Get out of your head!" Sorrel coached her.

Mirzam focused her eyes on her target.

Geena felt a suggestion, a tug, *run run run*. She barely escaped the chasm that Mirzam had created where she had been standing. She threw spell after spell at Mirzam. Stinging, slicing, burning, itching, and bashing spells. Mirzam was flung around like someone controlled by invisible strings. Geena approached to disarm Mirzam and end the fight when she saw a brick-like object flying toward her. It hit the floor beside Geena with a thud. She tried to cast a spell to move it away from her, but nothing happened. She heard Mirzam running toward her, no wand in hand. Geena tried another spell, but nothing.

Mirzam tackled her to the floor, Geena's wand flew out of her hand and rolled across the floor. Mirzam was trying to punch, scratch, and physically subdue Geena to win.

Geena immediately switched her technique for the fight. Dodging and hitting back at Mirzam. The two were rolling around on the floor, wanting to be on top of the other, when Geena's magic spoke to her again, *stay on the floor and move your head at the last second.*

Mirzam rolled herself on top of Geena and pulled her fist back to punch Geena. As her fist was coming down, Geena kept still, focusing on her hand, and when it was getting ready to connect with her face, Geena slung her head and torso to the side.

Mirzam cried out as her fist connected to the floor, blood coating her knuckles. Geena tossed Mirzam off and ran for her wand that had rolled towards Sorrel. As her fingers wrapped around her wand, familiar wood and groves settling in her fingers, she heard Mirzam storming towards her.

Without looking, she threw a spell over her shoulder, and after the sound of Mirzam hitting the floor, there was silence.

"So much for her invention," Sorrel started as he waved healers to check out Mirzam, "It doesn't like longer than five minutes."

————

"Surprisingly, our newest trainee is in better shape than almost all the wizards that have been here for a minute," Sorrel commented. Still keeping his distance from Geena like she was poison, he nodded in her direction. "All of you are still shit though."

What a compliment.

Sorrel turned and stomped off. He had had his fill of them after supervising the training session. Geena looked to the three other wizards for some indication of what to do next.

"Want a blackberry cobbler in exchange for me skipping training tomorrow?" Perseus' question caused Sorrel to stop as he reached the door, devious smirks on both of their faces.

"Make it two and we have a deal."

As Sorrel opened the door, he held it open for Dula and Juniper to walk in before he exited. Dula beckoned Geena and told Juniper to make sure the rest go where they are stationed for today.

Geena was perplexed by her separation from the other wizards whose companionship had helped her become less guarded, despite just meeting them. She still struggled with the faeries as a whole, especially those like Sorrel. She only knew Dula and Vinca, and she didn't know them that much since most conversations usually centered around her mother.

"We are taking you to Council, we will be asking you about the wizards chasing you," Vinca began, her voice not as light as it usually was. "We need you to be honest and as detailed as possible so we can help you."

"I don't know that much, they've just always ambushed me and I'm running for my life," Geena replied, voice shaking as her anxiety took over her exhaustion after training. Starting as a small flame, Geena anticipated her anxiety's transformation into a conflagration.

"Just tell us what you know," Dula said, her voice surprisingly gentle. "There'll be someone asking standard questions and we'll have some of our own." Her moment of comfort over, Dula hardened. Dula and Vinca gave Geena a small smile, and Geena tried to return it.

{ **5** }

CHAPTER FIVE:

Met with the grand greenery of the council room, Geena noticed the flowers were a different color than before. They were a blooming burnt orange that reminded her of a warm sunset. She stood as confidently as she could with so many eyes watching her. Other than the Kings and Queens, there were two large sections of faeries that lined each wall from the entrance to the thrones. Geena guessed there were at least a hundred fairies in here.

"State your name for the scribe," said a faerie that Geena remembered brought her the healing salve after Sorrel's thorns. She couldn't remember his name but any familiar face was comforting.

"Geena Bellows." She spoke as clearly as she could, hoping her voice wouldn't betray her nerves.

"State your age and magical origin."

"Uh..." Geena cleared her throat. "Nineteen. Half wizard and half faerie." She paused and looked to Vinca for guidance.

"Wizard and faerie confirmed," Orrin spoke with finality. He was aloof in his throne but even Geena could see his body tense as the noise of the crowd grew. He glared at the few faeries who voiced their thoughts in an angry manner. Orrin immediately stopped their chatter as he boomed, "She is my daughter. Her mother was a wizard. Geena's origins are wizard and faerie *confirmed*."

He paused to glare again at those who weren't happy with the statement. "If that is a problem, you will be taking that up with me."

The faeries along the sides of the Council room shrunk back from his stern tone. Orrin was not one to try your luck with it seems. Geena wondered if any of the kings and queens were faeries to try your luck with. *Most likely not.*

"Juniper indicated in her guard report that she saw you running away from a large group of wizards and after you put up a wall of fire to divide them from you, she approached and offered you help. Is what I said so far true?" The faerie asked, continuing his job as he led the discussion.

"Yes."

"After you accepted her help, she said that the two of you got a head start before you took the firewall down and you deflected the attacks while she led you to the faerie entrance. However, you entered the faerie land, Apatite, without her assistance, is that true?"

"Yes."

"There is your confirmation for the faerie origin," Dula interjected and nodded to the scribe, making sure they recorded her statement.

"Do you know who the wizards are that are chasing you?"

"I have a name, I think, but no confirmation," Geena responded warily.

"Geena, what is it?" Dula asked.

"I have heard a name that the wizards say when they are looking for me but I would be hiding." She took a breath before continuing, "Cepheus. They kept saying 'Cepheus will be mad' or 'Cepheus is going to kill us for letting her get away again."

Gasps came from every direction as the fae in attendance recognized the name and the fear associated with it.

"Cepheus is the leader of the group called the Score." The faerie in charge of the questioning relayed the information for Geena. "Thank you for your cooperation," the faerie said before asking the

Kings and Queens if they had any more questions so far. When they didn't, he continued. "Juniper also put in her report that she was impressed with your magical ability. Assuming you've been on the run for a while, where did you learn your skills?"

"My mom, Mia Bellows, taught me."

"Where is your mother now?"

"She got sick from a spell she was trying to make but before she passed she taught me what she could and gave me all of her books so I could learn more on my own."

"How did she become sick from a spell?" The question was from Vinca, voice gentle as she approached an obviously sensitive topic. Geena saw Dula lay her hand on top of Orrin's on the arm of his throne.

"She was working on a potion to help keep us in hiding. My mom was really good with creating new potions—this one back-fired though. It caused this bruise-like thing to spread from her fingers to the rest of her body. When the bruise reached an area those parts would stop working." Geena played with the necklace she was wearing as she spoke, it was the only thing her mother had given her that she was able to keep while being on the run. It was a simple chain with a silver pendant with the letter "M" engraved.

"Was she in pain?" Orrin asked, his voice breaking over the word 'pain.'

"I don't... No, I don't think so. She always seemed the same, just frustrated towards the end because I had to help her so much."

Orrin nodded and looked down towards his lap, but Geena recognized the look and knew he felt the absence of her mother almost as much as she did.

"Mia Bellows was a very skilled wizard. Confirmed," Orrin told the scribe.

"Confirmed," Dula repeated.

"Confirmed," Vinca echoed.

Surprisingly Sorrel and Cerise also murmured, "Confirmed."

"Are there any more questions for Geena before we dismiss this Council session?" When the faerie was met with silence, he nodded to Sorrel who sat in the middle of all the kings and queens.

"The Council is dismissed." Sorrel's voice boomed and the response was immediate as the faeries flushed out of the room with both speed and grace. When it was just Geena and the Kings and Queens, she collapsed to the floor, landing on her knees before sitting back on her feet. Before she could begin curling herself into a ball, one of the lingering faeries approached and held her as Geena focused on holding back her tears.

"Come on, Honey," Vinca said as came to Geena's side after a moment and dismissed the previous faerie. "Dula will you grab some food and some potions to help you sleep."

Vinca helped Geena stand and began walking her toward the exit, but Sorrel was blocking the doorway.

"Sorrel," Vinca growled in a warning.

He held up a hand at her before meeting Geena's eyes, "I apologize for calling you a 'half-breed.' Your mom was always kind to me, even when I wasn't to her." With that, he stepped away.

Seeing how emotionally spent Geena was, Vinca tugged lightly for her to continue walking. "Come on, let's get you back to your room."

————

Geena woke to someone knocking lightly at her door. After she mumbled a barely coherent "Come in," Percy opened the door carrying a tray with food.

"Breakfast already?" Geena sat up and looked at her watch.

"After lunch actually. Wanted to make you something, so I threw this together before heading to the gardens to help Mirzam and Meda gather some food," Percy said, setting the tray down on the left bedside table. "I didn't know what you'd like to drink so I just brought some water..." he trailed off.

Geena looked at the food and noticed it was blueberry pancakes with a bowl of blackberries.

"You remembered?" she said, trying to put real meaning behind her words, "Thank you. I really appreciate it."

"Anything for you, doll." Percy returned to his usual confidence and charm.

"Okay Percy, see you later."

"Overstepped? My bad." He put his hands up in surrender and made his way out. "Let me know if you need anything else." As much as Percy seemed to be an annoying flirt, he meant well.

$$\{\,6\,\}$$

CHAPTER SIX:

Would you like to have dinner together?

• Orrin

Geena turned the note over, the frayed edges of the paper kissing her fingertips. She debated how awkward the dinner would be. *Very* was all her brain would compute. "Inevitable," she mumbled to herself as she laced up the new boots Dula gave her for training. The leather was soft and practically molded to her foot like it was made only for her. Dula seemed to keep finding ways to spoil her.

Probably so I'll stay.

She was up before the rest of her house so she quietly threw to-gether a meal and went out of the porch to enjoy the calm and quiet morning. The floorboard barely squeaked under her light steps. She sat in one of the rocking chairs on the porch of the wizard hut and couldn't help but chuckle at the fact the houses were called huts. While nature was embedded through all the structures, the houses were an art form of their own. Since most faeries were air faeries, there was no shortage of wind chimes and other decorations that reminded Geena of a rotisserie chicken spinning on its skewer.

Too absorbed in the humor of replacing the decor with chickens, Geena didn't notice the faerie that approached until he was almost right beside her.

"Hey. Geena, right?" The voice caused her to jump, and as she was laughing it off and nodding to the boy she tried to remember his name.

"I'm sorry I don't remember your name. It's kind of hard with all the new people and new things." Geena held a hand out for the boy to shake.

"Mortimer." He shook her hand lightly. "We haven't been officially introduced, but you can call me Morty."

"Well Morty, what can I do for you?" Geena replied, taking another bite of her toast while waiting for his response.

"I just wanted to introduce myself to you in a moment that wasn't completely overwhelming like the Council meeting or bringing you healing paste."

Geena laughed lightly at his teasing and studied him as he stood at the porch steps. Fluffy brown hair and blazing golden eyes and tan skin speckled with patches of white.

Shaking her head to clear it, Geena said, "Sorry. I zoned out there for a second."

"It's okay. Were you distracted by my skin or my eyes?"

"Bold of you to assume I was distracted by you at all." She raised her eyebrows at him.

He laughed through his reply, "Right. You weren't what I expected."

"I'll take that as a compliment regardless of how you meant it."

"You should." He gestured to the chair near her. "May I join you?"

"Only if I can ask a bunch of questions," Geena told him, wanting to learn more about faeries and why some have some magical aspects to their appearance and they all are so different.

"Assuming no one has told you, fae identifiers are what give us away as not human," Mortimer spoke as if reading her mind and gestured to his eyes. Geena gave her full attention and nodded for him to continue. "My identifiers are my eyes and my wings." He displayed his wings for her briefly—*dragonfly wings*. "Vinca has the claws and the blue hue to her skin."

"Claws?!" Geena exclaimed.

"I know. She's one of the nicest creatures to ever exist, yet she has these haunting qualities that radiate power."

"The claws probably help with her gardening habit," Geena offered and was pleased when Mortimer nodded in reply.

"Orrin has his horns?" she asked.

"Yeah. Sorrel has his blue hair that changes hues in different lights, Cerise is a walking cherry, she's the faerie Queen of air..."

"Ah well a cherry blossom maybe. Just cherry is too extreme for her skin tone. It's quite beautiful with her sharp red hair," Geena interrupted and then gestured for Mortimer to continue.

"Cerise also has hair that changes hue. Dula, that spicy queen, has slanted silver eyes and matching butterfly wings."

"What decides the identifiers?"

"No one really knows," Mortimer said with a shrug.

Suddenly remembering her note this morning, Geena held up a finger to Mortimer to pause the conversation before holding up the note. "Would you mind taking my reply to Orrin? I don't know how communication works here yet and I wouldn't know where to find him."

Mortimer laughed at her, not in a mean manner. He whistled four sharp staccato notes and waited. After a few moments, Geena was met with blazing wings.

"This is a firebird. The result of some potion Vinca made a few decades ago. They are pretty nifty when it comes to communication though. Just tell them what you want them to do and in the time it takes to blow out a candle, they've done it."

Geena was starstruck. Amazed by the wondrous colors of red and orange. She held out the note carefully and the bird took hold of it with its beak, flames never making purchase on the paper.

"Could you take this to Orrin please?" Geena asked nicely and stood up slowly, not wanting to frighten the bird. It chirped in response and took off. In less than a second or so, she lost sight of the firebird. "Wow."

"Wow is right." Mortimer stood beside her now.

"So why would I be distracted by your skin?" Geena asked.

"Vitiligo."

"That's normal, you know. Humans even have that. I think there's even a few famous models too. Can't remember with being on the run for so long," Geena said, her voice fading toward the end.

"It's not very common in faeries."

"Oh. Sorry if I offended you, wasn't my intention." She gave him a smile that she hoped conveyed her feelings and he matched it, but it didn't seem as genuine.

————

"THEY SENT A MISSION!" Percy interrupted the girls' quiet afternoon when he skidded through the doorway, papers shaking in his hands and a crazed look in his eyes.

"Are you serious?" Meda put down her book on the couch and stood to take the papers from them.

Geena studied them as Meda read with Percy over her shoulder. Meda mumbled the words quietly to herself, stopped, groaned, and then began reading again. Mirzam and Geena looked at each other in confusion.

"Fuck," Meda's voice was low but it conveyed her anxieties.

"Fuck is right." That was all Percy said as he walked over to the loveseat and crashed down into it beside Geena.

"We have to steal faerie artifacts back from The Score," Meda stated, handing the paper to Mirzam who quickly immersed herself in the words and began scribbling ideas on a notepad.

"The Score?" Geena looked at Percy. "Like the mafia group that has been trying to kill me?"

Meda responded, "Yes and also the mafia that," she pointed out between her and Percy, "our Dad is the leader of."

Geena's spine sprung straight and the other wizards saw the fear in her eyes as she scooted as far as possible from Percy as the loveseat would allow.

"They didn't tell her?" Mirzam spoke for the first time in hours, her voice breaking. They all looked at Geena who shook her head.

"Do I—does that mean—the mission—am I..." Geena started.

"The mission requires all four of us and a faerie escort to get us in and out of Apatite," Meda supplied, looking at Geena with eyes full of pity. *The faeries shouldn't force her to do this*, Meda thought to herself. *They shouldn't force children to fight against their own parents either.*

"If it makes the situation better, the only reason we were able to escape," Mirzam gestured between herself and the twins, "is because we faked our deaths. We left because we hated it there, and blew up a whole building to cover up our not-so-dead bodies." Her voice was light as always, regardless of how dark the statement she gave.

"What do we do now?" Percy asked.

"I plan," Mirzam said, "you cook, and Meda will help Geena get ready for her dinner."

Geena scoffed, "It's not a date. It's dinner with my biological dad who I have never talked to."

"I think getting ready is more to keep your nerves settled," Mirzam replied.

"I could use the distraction as well," Meda said with a shrug and a pitied glance toward Geena.

————

Orrin had arrived on the porch of the hut when the sun had just begun to fall behind the trees. The sunlight that peaked through the leaves made his pale hair glow, giving the illusion of a halo around his curled horns. He waited patiently outside until Geena was ready and began walking with her to wherever they were having their dinner.

Their walk was quiet, observing the majestic scenery more than interacting with each other. Geena felt like this should be awkward but the energy of the land was so hypnotizing and soothing to her nerves tonight. She was absorbed in the way the lights flickered off the leaves, making them almost glow. A breeze wafted through the greenery and Geena was amazed as it looked like the plants were breathing. While she was still dreading this conversation with Orrin, *her father*, she internalized that serenity to get her through the evening.

"I like your necklace by the way. Your mom loved jewelry, and I'm pretty sure that was her favorite." Orrin gestured vaguely with a shake of his hand before he opened the door to one of the more modest huts and held the door for her. "After you."

Geena was met with cool shades of blue, purple, and green. In spite of the chill tone of the colors, the house was warm and felt like a hug from an old friend. She assumed that Orrin lived here considering the hints of water that seems to exist everywhere.

"I'm starving," Orrin clapped his hands together, whether to break the silence or release some tension, Geena couldn't tell but she laughed lightly as she followed him into another room where a table was set for two.

They ate their meal of roasted chicken and mashed potatoes in soothing silence. Geena did not mind, she wanted time to get used to being around him before opening the Pandora's box that was their relationship or lack thereof. Geena felt her magic reaching out, testing to see if it would react on its own and warn her if things went south. So far, her magic agreed with most people she had encountered, the only uncertain ones were Mortimer and Sorrel. Then again Geena had been overwhelmed with all of the new people in a foreign place. She was immediately drawn to Orrin though, from their first interaction she felt the pull of her magic wanting to go to him. Geena could probably navigate her way through the foreign fae land, Apatite, to find Orrin by simply following the tugging of her magic. Her mother impressed upon Geena to trust her magic always, that it will sense danger before anything else. *"Magic is the purest, untainted version of yourself. Trust it and protect it the way it does for you."* Lost in thoughts of her mother, she didn't realize she had cleaned her plate until her fork scraped against the plate, drawing her back to reality.

When Orrin had finished his last bite, Geena took a deep breath attempting to slow her racing heart, or at least calm it so it didn't beat through her chest.

"Wine?" Orrin stood suddenly. "I think we need wine if we're actually going to talk successfully." He retrieved two glasses and a bottle. "Do you want to talk here? Or we can go to the living room, has comfier chairs."

Geena agreed to the latter option—if she was going to do this, she was going to be comfortable.

"I'm sorry to hear about your mom's passing," Orrin said as he handed her a full glass of wine.

She smiled sadly in return, "I'm sorry you lost someone you loved too. It's nice to know Mom was loved."

"Love," Orrin corrected her. "There will never come a time when I don't love her, not even her death will prevent that." He offered a crooked smile, realizing that was probably a lot to hear at once.

"So you're my dad who I didn't know existed until just the other day. How do you make up for so many years? How do I be a daughter to a stranger?"

"You're not twenty-one, are you?" Orrin looked concerned. "Give the wine back, you're not of age."

Geena couldn't stop her eruption of laughter. "You're serious? Faerie's have a drinking age? "

"This conversation won't go anywhere if the two of us are worried about our nerves." Geena took another long sip.

"Faerie's don't really have a set drinking age but I know humans do." Orrin looked to the floor. "Sorry, I kind of tried to make up for almost two decades in one second. I guess I went into parental mode there."

"Maybe we could be friends first, yeah?" Geena smiled at him and was met with a small nod.

"I'd like that."

"How'd you meet my mom?"

"Saved her life, and I kid you not, she then had to save my ass." A smile spread over Orrin's face as he told Geena of how he was supposed to be foraging for potion ingredients but he decided to try and buy them instead and saved her mother from drowning as her leg was caught in some vines and she wasn't a strong enough swimmer to manage it. Then as her mom walked with Orrin back to where she needed to be, wizards ambushed them and said Orrin's horns would make for good *spoils* or decor. He ended up being more beat up than her mom, so she helped stitch him up but before she left he asked if she would like to meet again. "By the grace of every higher power, Mia agreed. We were friends for a long time before it evolved into anything more."

"How come you weren't around? I could've grown up here," Geena said as she filled both of their glasses, finishing off the bottle.

"Your mom and I decided it would be best. Wizards are a lot more hostile to faeries than faeries are to wizards. To the best of my knowledge, you are the only half-faerie/half-wizard ever. Some of the faeries here though weren't very welcoming of Mia. Dula and Vinca adored her. I obviously did... Sorrel just ignored her mostly, which is as good as it gets with him. Cerise, however, loathed your mother. Never figured out why, but she would always plan these little tricks that wouldn't harm Mia much but when we found out she was pregnant I couldn't risk Cerise finding out and hurting Mia or you." He sighed and ran his hand through the hair between his horns. "So I decided to play the role of a deadbeat dad and 'left' your mom. We tried to write to each other but that became too risky after you were born. I only heard from her once after we cut off communication, I think I have it around here somewhere." Orrin stood and walked over to the end table near the fireplace and rummaged through the drawers until he found what he was looking for.

"Here it is, her last note to me." He handed it to Geena and as she unfolded it a picture fell in her lap. She read the note before looking at the picture.

"*Geena Calendula Bellows. Loves to swim and look broody like someone else I know. Love you now and always.*"

The picture was of her and her mother in front of a Christmas tree display, laughing as the snow fell around them.

Geena recalled, "That was the first time I ever saw snow. We weren't on the run yet, I was about five or six. We only started hiding a lot when I was seven or eight. She died when I was eighteen." Geena folded the note around the picture carefully and handed it back to Orrin and sat beside him on the couch.

"What happened the first time the two of you were attacked?" Orrin asked before taking a sip from his glass, "you don't have to tell me. I'm just curious how she managed with you so young at the time."

Geena sighed, "I'll tell you."

It happened around the middle of the day, and the heat was suffocating. There was music playing that Geena could hear her mom humming along to. Mia was in the kitchen fixing lunch when Geena came up and wrapped her arms around Mia's leg, too small to reach higher.

"Lunch will be ready soon, Geena."

"Momma, something feels bad."

Mia put down the sandwich she was fixing and bent down to be eye level with Geena. "What's wrong, honey?" Mia held Geena's face in her hands, looking for any cuts or bruises.

"I'm not hurt."

"Can you tell me what feels bad?"

"The tingly thing we talked about. The magic tingly thing." Geena mumbled, looking at her feet.

"Geena," Mia started.

"*You told me to trust it and it will keep me safe. My magic is doing the weird tingle.*"

"*What do you think it is trying to tell you?*"

"*To run from bad people.*" Geena said.

Mia was confused. She had noticed that Geena was sensitive to her magic and would listen to it without thought. Geena's reflexes were sharp for being so young; almost impossibly, she had avoided many accidents around the house by either getting out of the way or catching things before they fell and broke. Mia knew that children were more susceptible to their magical instincts, but Geena was hypersensitive and knew things that made little sense. Mia's attention snapped back to Geena when she grabbed her shoulders, a panicked look in her young eyes.

"*Mommy, we need to go.*"

Mia did not have many things in their small house, with a bathroom, kitchenette, and a tiny bedroom. It only took minutes to pack all of the essentials her and Geena would need to be alright for a few days. Geena was right beside Mia as they both carried an armful of bags and tossed them in the trunk of the old car that Mia had.

"*Do you need my help getting in your car seat?*" Mia asked.

"*No. Just drive.*"

As Mia got into the driver's seat and put her seatbelt on, her magical instincts began warning her that something was wrong; danger was coming. Mia could only think of one person who would mean harm to her, Cepheus. He was probably the leader of the Score now, considering how fast he was climbing the ranks before Mia left to go live in Apatite.

She got the car keys out of her pocket, looked back to make sure Geena was situated, and started the car. The driveway left a cloud of dust as Mia hurried towards the road. After a few minutes, Mia turned up the radio and noticed that one of her favorite songs was playing.

"*Geena, it's the Bee Gees!*" Mia looked in the rearview mirror to see a sincere look on Geena's face. "*What's wrong honey?*"

"*Boom.*" Geena replied.

In the rearview and side mirrors of her car, Mia saw a cloud of smoke coalescing in the mushroom shape about where their house was located. Tears collected in Mia's eyes, but she quickly wiped them away to be strong for Geena in case she was upset.

"Momma, turn the music louder. I wanna sing."

Mia did and just kept driving. Creating as much distance between the explosion and wherever they would stop next. Mia knew that they would be running from now on, escaping the fatal fate Cepheus had planned for her and her daughter.

The fire crackled in the fireplace and Geena's eyes felt heavy from the wine and the conversation. With her magic surrounding her in a blanket of warmth, she felt calm and safe. Geena leaned into the sensation she hadn't felt in so long. Her head had fallen on Orrin's shoulder without her realizing it, and he leaned his head on top of hers.

"She never loved anyone else. Told me her heart was only big enough for two," Geena mumbled before slowly drifting to sleep.

Orrin carried her to his room and put her in bed. "I'll take care of you, if you'll let me," he said as he pushed some hair out of her face before he grabbed an extra pillow from the bed and retired to the couch in the living room.

{ 7 }

CHAPTER SEVEN:

Still not used to being able to sleep soundly, Geena was up early and sneaking out of Orrin's house before the sun was up. She left a note for him saying she had a good time and suggested more dinners together. Geena was surprised at how awkward the evening wasn't. She kept waiting for it to be overwhelming, but more than anything she just felt like she got a piece of her mom back.

By the time she made it back to the wizard hut the sun was washing the landscape in a golden morning glow. She quietly made her way to the kitchen where she found Percy singing softly to himself as he made breakfast for the house.

"He sings and he cooks," Geena said, leaning against the doorway. Percy jumped slightly and turned around with a smile and a mumbled good morning.

"Well, it's all in the balance of things," he said as he began cutting up some strawberries. "Meda helps gather things from the garden and deflate my ego, Mirzam plans all the attacks and takes inventory of all food and stuff so I know what I can cook. And I," Percy bowed to her, "the lovely Perseus cooks the food for the ladies."

"Do I come into play?" Geena stole a few berries after her question.

Percy looked at her like she had three heads. "Duh, we just haven't figured out how to exploit your gifts domestically. For fighting, you're our number one gal." Percy began piling food on four plates. "You should've seen the plans Mirzam marked down last night. Geena, you're plan A to G, then it's all up to my poor fighting skills to save the day."

She laughed. "Well, it would help if you weren't always bribing Sorrel to get out of training."

"I have no regrets."

"Do you ever?"

"Good morning guys!" Mirzam bounced in and sat down at the table. "Did I spook you? Sorry. How was dinner with Orrin? I hope it went well. I was a little worried about you last night. Well, when I wasn't drafting plans. I can't wait for you to see them!"

"Mirzam, you're amazing, I love you, but your brain is the only one that operates this fast in the morning." Percy laughed at her.

"The only brain that operates that fast, period," Geena added, earning a high five from Percy and a slight snicker from Mirzam.

"Andromeda should be up soon, I was a little louder than normal getting ready this morning."

"Wait, you and Meda share a room?" Geena asked Mirzam. "Did I take a room from one of you?"

"No, no, no! Meda and I have always shared a room. Neither of us like to room alone."

"That and Perc is the worst snorer ever." Meda waddled in, looking the least put together since Geena had met her.

"Nice jammies, Meda. I think I have a set of loungewear that looks just like that," Percy said.

"It's because these are yours, dickhead," she shot back.

Geena laughed at the siblings' antics and she felt something she hadn't felt in a long time, hadn't felt since her mom passed—at home. Maybe this place and the people around could be her new home and her new hodge-podge family.

———

Geena was amazed by the way Mirzam had modified a spell that made projections of the area and building that the wizards would need to get into to steal the artifacts back. Geena poked the top of the projection and pulled it up, which made the outer walls come up so you could see the interior layout of the building.

"Mirzam, you amaze me more every day." Vinca approached the projection and studied it more closely.

"What's all the mission for again?" Geena asked.

"The artifacts of fae, they contain magic that protects faeries and our powers. Without them, we grow weaker." Vinca explained, walking around the projection, "The main reason we agreed to hold asylum for the wizards is they came to us, saying that they knew where the artifacts were and that they wanted to help get them back to us."

"We knew they were stolen but we didn't know where they were at the time." Orrin added.

The five faerie leaders and the wizards gathered around to review Mirzam's plan of attack. Geena was more than thoroughly impressed; she hadn't seen magic tweaked and manipulated so well since her mother passed. The look she shared with Orrin told her two things—he agreed with her, and Mirzam's brilliance was a normal occurrence. Mirzam began laying out where the group would start and where they would need to split up to be as fast as possible.

"Mirzam, where did you get all of this information?" Geena asked.

"You'd be surprised how much stuff is online these days, blueprints included," she responded.

After some debate, it was agreed that Dula would go with the wizards since she was the most skilled for such a fast-paced mission, and as had Dula said, "Vinca lacks the subtle touch to sneak around and we have no need for a blazing inferno in our company."

Sorrel played with Vinca's hair as she glared at Dula playfully but opted to lean into Sorrel and listen to the rest of the plan.

Geena watched Sorrel and Vinca carefully for a moment, the peaceful look in their eyes, and maybe even a slight smile on Sorrel. Sorrel usually only displayed this softness for Percy's cobblers. Cerise left, no longer needing to be a part of this conversation since Dula was chosen to accompany the group, pictures on the wall rattling as she slammed the door.

Percy leaned toward Geena and whispered, "Always so touchy." The two of them held their laughs in and smirked at each other before turning their attention to the escape routes that Mirzam was now going over. Apparently, there were a significant number of escape routes, which was good if something went wrong, but made the meeting last a lot longer than they all originally thought. After a while, Sorrel left because he was hungry and no one wanted to deal with his sour mood, except for Vinca who followed him out with a smile. Which just left the four wizards, Dula, and Orrin.

Orrin gave suggestions every now and then to the tentative plan that Mirzam had put together but she only accepted one or two of the proposed changes, showing how the other amendments would lead to failure. Dula and Meda just observed, watching the golden dots that represented them going in and getting out of the building.

"What are we even looking for? What do the artifacts look like?" Geena finally asked, realizing that she did not know what the artifacts were.

Mirzam, prepared for such a question, handed her a small stack of papers that had figures and carvings displayed on them. "A goblet, a chest, and a scroll."

Geena studied the pictures and tried to decipher what they were but the figures kept morphing in and out, first a cup and then an old thick book. Dula and Orrin noticed her confusion but did not say anything.

Meda however, said, "Surely you have seen a goblet before?"

Geena's eyes snapped up and met Dula's and she deciphered the message the queen was trying to convey. *They can't see what you can.*

They're not supposed to. She glanced at Orrin and was met with the same look.

"Yeah, I was just trying to figure out the writings on the cup," Geena replied before the others became suspicious.

"I've been trying to decode those for weeks. Quite tricky, it's a different grammar structure and the words don't translate perfectly," Mirzam offered and asked if anyone had any questions. Geena just asked if she could keep the pictures for a bit, so she could remember what the artifacts looked like before the mission. "Right well, I think we should do this on a night where the moon isn't so bright, so we'll go in a few weeks since the full moon is coming up and we need the extra time to train." Mirzam looked to the two remaining leaders for confirmation and received two approving nods.

————

"Why can't they tell what the artifacts are?" Geena asked Orrin later that night as they had dinner together again. "What are they really?"

"Some protection magic the original faeries put on it. A crystal, a book, and the scroll, which is the only one that doesn't change its appearance to non-fae. You have to be fae to recognize what they really are...Do you want any of the sauce?" Orrin offered both information and the food to her, she only accepted the former.

"I was thinking about brewing some potions in between training so we can stock up for our mission," Geena said.

"Oh that'll be good, I'm sure Vinca and Dula would love the company."

"Well that's the thing, Dula wants me to get in touch with 'my faerie side'," Geena said, putting air quotes around the words. "I was able to start one potion the other week but it completely exhausted me. Dula thinks you might be able to help me."

"As flattered as I am, Dula is well-aware that I am absolute shit at potions," Orrin said with a laugh that was joined by Geena's.

"Yes, I've heard some stories of your attempts," she chuckled, "but Dula thinks that you being around will help me provoke my faerie magic."

"I suppose that makes sense. I'll do whatever you need me to do; I'll see if I can find any books on dormant faerie magic to help."

"Thank you Orrin, it means a lot."

"Well, we're family. I know I missed years but we have each other now and I will do everything in my power for you to be safe and happy, always."

"Would it be weird to hug you right now?"

"I think it is perfectly normal for a daughter to hug her dad." Orrin stood, the legs of his chair scuffed on the hardwood and he walked over to Geena and engulfed her in a hug.

Geena hadn't had any physical affection in so long that she was sure she had a death grip on Orrin, squeezing all the air out of him. He didn't complain or pull away and neither did she. So they stood there holding each other for a while. As her magic wrapped around them, Geena wondered if he could feel it. She reveled in the feeling of safety and protection that came with Orrin.

"I'm sorry," he eventually mumbled, still holding her close.

Her reply was muffled from his embrace. "Why? You have nothing to be sorry for."

He sighed and finally pulled away enough to see her face but still held her. She noticed he had some tears gathering. "You shouldn't have had to be alone. I should've gone with you and Mia. I should've kept you here, kept you safe, done something."

Geena tucked herself back into his embrace, thinking that maybe if she held him tight enough it would keep her from breaking or fuse together a bond that had years' worth of hugs.

"I think that you did the best for what you and Mom knew at the time. I know how much she loved me and even though our time has been brief it has been filled with nothing but love." Geena pulled away again. Orrin's tears had escaped now. "I think Mom would be happy that we found each other and that we're trying." Orrin could only nod as he wiped away some of the tears from his face.

"I think, no, I *know* she'd be so proud of you," he said, looking earnestly at Geena. "I'll help you with whatever you need with your potions, just tell me when. But maybe don't ask me to hand you ingredients, I mess those up all the time."

Even in their grief of lost time and the absence of Geena's mom, the smiles on their faces were hopeful and happy. They felt as if they had found something that they did not even know was missing until that hug. Geena promised to herself that she would always hug Orrin, her dad, whenever she had the chance.

{ **8** }

CHAPTER EIGHT:

Having an extra few weeks to prepare for the mission was a relief for the wizards; they all wanted to train, but Geena wanted to keep building back all of the muscle she had lost while being on the run and not having secure food sources. She was pleased to not look as skeletal anymore but wasn't used to all the new energy that came from having routine meals. In the mornings, she would leave the hut just before sunrise and run around the faerie land, both to get in the best shape for the upcoming mission, and because she never tired of the beautiful landscape. Exploring it daily helped ease Geena's anxiety that told her she needed to keep moving and not stay in one place so long. When she got back from her run, Percy would have breakfast ready for the house. On the fourth day of this routine, she ran into Juniper and Morty.

"Geena!" Juniper called out and waved her to come over to one of the market stands, where Juniper was purchasing some food. "How have you been? I've been meaning to check on you."

"I've been alright. The food is good so I think I'll stick around." Geena and Juniper laughed.

"Morty and I were just switching guard shifts," Juniper said.

"I thought you worked in the Council?" Geena asked Mortimer, unsure if it was normal for faeries to have multiple jobs.

"I do, but the Council doesn't meet every day, so I'm part of the Guard as well," he explained.

"Oh okay! Sometimes I feel so crazy for not knowing basic things around here," Geena said.

Morty and Juniper met her comment with laughter. "Are you kidding?" Morty asked, "You should have been here when the other wizards arrived. The twins kept to themselves for a while but the other was blasting questions left and right. It was annoying as hell."

"Morty, shut up. They are all nice, Mirzam just has a thirst for knowledge," Juniper said pointedly, almost defensive of Mirzam.

"Eh, wizards are finicky. Never know what tricks they are going to pull."

"Well then, as a wizard, I should get going to plan more tricks to pull on unsuspecting faeries, shouldn't I?" Geena said and turned away intending to continue her run. She heard Morty say something to Juniper quickly before he was grabbing her shoulder trying to stop her.

"Wait Geena, I didn't mean it like that," Morty said apologetically.

"How did you mean it then?"

"I don't know. I'm just not fond of the three of them acting like they are better than everyone else and not helping out," Morty offered with a careless shrug.

Geena stood up as straight as she could, hands on her hips. "They help out every day. They may not help with the Council or Guard but they are in the gardens or cooking or doing something."

"I'm sorry. I didn't mean to hurt your feelings," Morty said.

"I'm not concerned about my feelings." Geena's hair started sparking towards the ends, her magic pulsating with her anger, pushing her to defend her friends, boiling up telling Geena to *protect them!* "I'm concerned about how my friends are being talked about behind their backs." She took a step towards Morty. "They are good people and have been nothing but welcoming and kind to me since I've gotten here. So do not speak badly of them, Mortimer."

"Morty."

"Mortimer!" Geena finally raised her voice from her stoic tone, hair sparking wildly. "I only call my friends by a nickname. Have a good day, Mortimer." She spit out his name and he flinched as he could feel the burn of the venom she spoke with her hair almost an inferno as she began running again.

With each stomp of her foot, Geena released more and more energy. Anger out as she landed on the earth and exhaled, and peace as she inhaled and picked up her foot to move further away from the conflict. She ran and ran until she was about to dry heave, so she decided to sit in the clovers that were more abundant in the faerie land than grass was in the normal world.

Combing her fingers through the clusters of clovers, she didn't notice the firebird until it was flying around her hand. She gently took the note it delivered and the bird accepted her gentle scratch of its head before purring a collection of notes and flying away.

I get really nervous around you and say things I don't mean. I'm sorry for talking badly about your friends. Let me apologize and make it up to you over dinner.

Just think about it?

   • *Mortimer, hoping to be called Morty again*

Geena agreed on one condition, that the dinner was with the other wizards too.

———

The dinner did not go well. Meda and Mirzam tried to keep the peace but the second Mortimer made a jab about Mirzam's "inability to shut up", Percy was on the offense, defending his sister and their friend like his life depended on it. Mortimer did not back down and began throwing vicious insults about Percy and Meda's family, which weren't tolerated when it went past their father. The night ended with

Meda throwing a dinner knife at Mortimer's head and Geena's magic acting out, destroying all the glass in the room. As Geena all but dragged Mortimer out of the house, he turned to her with anger in his eyes and spoke calmly, "I had hope for you, but you are more filth than you are fae."

Geena did not reply to his statement with words, in fact she didn't speak again until late that night when Mirzam asked what happened since they all heard a loud bang soon after Geena and Mortimer went outside. Geena waved it off, saying "Nothing crazy." She hugged her mug to her chest as her smile grew confident, "Just took the trash out."

{ **9** }

CHAPTER NINE:

The full moon came and went quickly, leaving the wizards on edge in anticipation for the mission. Surprisingly, Percy quit skipping training days. Which left Geena not feeling so guilty when Dula pulled her out to work on potions, trying to inspire her "fae side to come out and play." However, Geena had been unsuccessful so far. As promised Orrin always came when they worked on it, although he kept to the farthest corner away from any ingredients, his nose tucked in a book trying to find ways to help.

Geena had only successfully done one faerie potion by the time it came for the mission, it exploded five minutes after she finished it. Orrin informed her that he had never done anything that bad. In his gloating, he didn't see the stirrer that Geena threw at him. He only laughed as it bounced off of his shoulder. Geena joined him in laughter when they noticed that some of the exploded potion had landed on Dula's hair, covering it in bubbling slime that shifted between cobalt blue and a sick green. "I think I'm going to start getting ready for the mission tonight," Dula said as she walked out of the potions lab gracefully, ignoring the disarray of her appearance.

"Let's get you some food before you need to start getting ready," Orrin said as he helped put away labeled bottles, knowing better to try and mess with anything else. He scribbled a note quickly and whistled for a firebird, "Take this to Vinca, please."

"Can we do something light for dinner?" Geena asked as she pulled her hair into a ponytail, ignoring the sparks that were popping off her hair. "Can you cook? I know Percy has been fixing most of the meals we've had."

"Soup or oatmeal is all I know how to cook. What are you feeling inclined to?"

"Carrot soup?"

Orrin froze for a second before he looked at her, a tight smile on his face. "You're in luck, that happens to be my specialty. You can thank your mother for that."

———

Geena was casting weight-lightening spells on the plethora of knives and other weapons she had on her person in case she lost her wand. While she was capable of doing magic without a wand, she hadn't practiced enough and it would quickly tire her. Mirzam noticed and had started to do the same for herself and Meda. Percy was prepping in his own way that slightly disturbed the girls but helped ease the tension.

Unbothered by his mocking audience, Percy continued his performance of "You Should Be Dancing" by the Bee-Gees, which Geena only knew from her mother's affinity for human music, until Dula appeared with Orrin, who quickly silenced Percy with a look. Percy had the sense to look apologetic as he stopped.

"Everyone remember the plan? And the back-up plan after that?" Dula spoke with authority. At moments like this Geena could easily understand why she was one of the faerie rulers. She could see the unstoppable force Dula exuded and the unmovable ground she stood on.

"Don't try to re-group unless necessary until you are back on fae ground," Orrin reminded them. "We have extra faeries on guard tonight in case everything goes to shit. There is also a 'decoy' group of faeries to draw out most of the wizards, since they always take the chance to hunt us down. Juniper will be stationed where you are supposed to re-enter. B-But for all the higher powers that exist, please don't die."

"That was so inspiring, I think I might cry," Percy barely managed to say before Meda silenced him with a swift smack to the back of his head.

"He acts like this before every mission when he's nervous. He's not excited to visit what used to be home." Meda told Geena. "It's annoying as hell but he sobers up when we actually get underway."

————

The building was barely visible in the distance from their vantage point. Geena could see where there were supposed to be streetlights, but none were lit. Mirzam was a little bummed that the visibility was higher than she was anticipating but Dula told them to give her a minute and it should be better.

Clouds smoothly rolled in and the stars disappeared one by one until they could barely see what was in front of them. Dula was breathing heavily, focusing her power to keep coalescing water droplets into clouds. Geena gave her an energy potion when Dula announced that the clouds should hold for almost half of an hour.

"If this runs smoothly, we should only need fifteen minutes tops," Mirzam said as she gave everyone a bracelet. "If you get into trouble, tap it three times and it will take you back to the forest where we are supposed to meet up with Juniper to get back to the fae land."

"Everyone ready?" Dula asked as she pulled her sleeve back down to cover the bracelet. When they all nodded, they split up to approach from different angles like they had planned. The building reminded Geena of a prison she had seen in a movie, although the fence topped with barbed wire was not as hard to get through as she expected.

Geena's entrance was smooth up until the point where the door, long out of use, screeched in protest to her moving it. Freezing in anticipation of an attack, she relaxed after a minute of silence and continued, figuring that by now either no one heard her or one of the others was creating a distraction. She cleared the hallway of a threat, knocking out two guards that were patrolling the area, before checking every room for the artifacts. After clearing the floor, she descended into the basement. On the dark stairs, she didn't notice her foot caught on a string. The second she took another step, sirens began blaring and every single inch of the room was bathed in bright light. Geena ducked her head to avoid the glare.

She heard a spell cut through the air and immediately went on the offensive. Hearing thundering steps from above her, she threw spell after spell at the few wizards coming down the stairs. When grunts became cries and screams, the wooden steps began to creak under her weight. Silencing everyone in the room with a spell, she hid under the staircase between two dressers in storage, using the dust cloth protecting them to cover herself. At the brief glimpse of a silver butterfly wing, Geena came out of her hiding spot, making some noise to not frighten Dula. Geena gave a silent thumbs up as a question and when Dula returned the gesture, the two went about searching the room for the artifacts.

"Dula, I found the artifact! Can you help me open the chest? We need to make sure there's not a tracker or bomb on it." Geena whispered. Barely hearing Dula walk over to her she was surprised to see her right behind when she turned to ask again. Instead of the normal and loving silver eyes that she was used to, she was met with red. When Geena looked back towards the chest, it was opened and had a note inside.

Run.

Before she could move, Dula had a tight grip on Geena's shoulders. Geena grunted under the pressure of fingers puncturing her skin and fought to take a full breath. She began coughing, trying to clear her lungs for air, instead it was water. The redness in Dula's eyes intensified as Geena struggled to breathe. Geena's confusion gave way to panic when she realized Dula was flooding her lungs, and she was doing it on purpose. Opting to ask for forgiveness instead of permission

Geena gripped her wand tightly, feeling the familiar soft wood, using it to ground herself before casting her first non-verbal spell.

The shift was immediate but weaker than Geena needed to gain her wits, but Dula wasn't expecting gravity to reverse itself, so when what was up was coming down and what was on the ground began rising to the ceiling, Geena expelled all the water she could from her lungs and kicked out at Dula's abdomen, pushing her away. Able to get in a deep breath, Geena cast a barrier of fire between them and began to scale the stairs.

"Meda! Help!" Geena screamed for the first person she could think of while she could breathe and cast a few protective spells to make her more resistant to any attacks, both faerie and wizard. Geena did everything she could to put objects in Dula's path to stop her murderous pursuit, however, Dula could fly and Geena did not have the time or the strength to block her from ceiling to the floor. Hearing fire sizzling into steam, Geena sped around the building even faster than she could think.

"Mirzam! Percy!" Geena almost had made it to the door where she had entered when water surrounded her and thrashed her around like she was stuck in a wave. Her head struck a corner of a door and the water began to darken as the pain of it resonated, making spots appear in her vision. When she was released from the water she felt like a flopping fish struggling to breathe and almost cried in relief when she heard Meda and Percy distract Dula. When Geena felt hands on her shoulders, she instantly began to fight away from it but calmed a little at the sight of Mirzam, casting dozens of spells around her.

"Tell me what happened so I can undo the curse Dula is under," Mirzam said calmly, holding pressure over the bleeding spots on Geena's shoulders.

Between gasps, Geena rasped out, "Chest." Leaning on Mirzam to try to get her feet properly under her, she croaked again, "Basement." That must have been enough for Mirzam to know what to do when she tucked Geena into a corner and ran towards the basement. Meda and Percy were fighting in tandem, picking up where the other left off and deflecting Dula's attacks. Geena held her wand close to her and cast warming spells to make it more difficult for Dula to fully coalesce vapor in the air into water. Once she had done that she scrambled for a faerie healing potion in her pocket and swallowed it.

Geena saw Mirzam emerge from the basement dragging a body with a similar head injury to Geena's. Looking at Geena between spells, Mirzam began altering the appearance of the wounded wizard. Geena watched as a burly bald man's features slowly morphed into a mirror vision of herself before Mirzam drew Dula's attention to "Geena."

"Looking for her?" Mirzam asked calmly, offering "Geena" to Dula as you'd offer a guest at your house a drink. Dula's smile was evil as she lurched for "Geena." Between the coughs for air and the pool of blood gathering around "Geena," they all realized that Dula was drowning the wizard while simultaneously stabbing her to death. With each ounce of blood, Dula's eyes faded from their vibrant, raging red back to their normal cool silver. Until Dula gasped with horror and jumped off of the body, whimpering at the sight of her shaking bloodied hands.

"Geena?" Was all Dula managed to squeak out before she fainted.

{ **10** }

CHAPTER TEN:

Geena woke to hushed murmurs around her. She tried to decipher what was being said before opening her eyes but it was too muffled. Blinking, she went to sit up but was met with gentle, but firm hands on her shoulders.

"Sitting up will make it harder for the potion to drain all the water in your lungs," Orrin spoke, eyes grazing over Geena, checking to make sure every wound was tended to.

"Is everyone okay? Did we get the artifacts?"

Orrin's eyes filled with sadness. "Percy, Andromeda, and Mirzam had a few minor injuries that were an easy fix," he sighed. "Dula is okay physically. We've had to keep her sedated. Whatever curse was in that chest has had some residual effects on her, so she'll panic and get violent."

"Can't you just remove the water in my lungs?" Geena asked.

"Not without risk. I can't tell the natural level of moisture in someone's lungs. I'd be just as likely to hurt you as leaving the fluid in your lungs would." He ran his hands over his face. "They got the cup and the scroll. The chest is the last one of them but Mirzam has to figure out the curse that was put on it because if any fae are around it, they try to kill whoever opened the chest."

{ 60 }

"That explains Dula's attack, she must feel awful." Geena managed to sit up despite Orrin's efforts to stop her. He rose from his chair beside her and helped adjust the pillows to support her.

"In between sedation and murderous bouts, she screams to whoever is around to prove to her you are okay and alive." Orrin fell back into his chair, "She'll be alright eventually once Mirzam figures out how to completely destroy the spell. Once you were stable, I went to Dula and told her you were okay and that no one was upset with her, that I was not upset with her."

"I'm not upset either, I just want her to be okay." Geena choked on her next words, "When Mirzam offered a fake me to Dula and she attacked it, she snapped out of it and she sounded like she was in so much pain."

"She was one of your mother's best friends and you're named after her, I'm sure she felt like she not only failed you but failed Mia too."

Geena traced Orrin's face for a lie, to find nothing but truth. "I'm named after her?"

Orrin's chuckle was coarse but had some levity to it. "Middle name. What do you think 'Dula' is short for?"

Geena smiled sadly and whispered to herself, "Calendula."

————

On a rainy Tuesday morning, five days after the mission, Mirzam figured out how to undo the curse and remove it from the chest. She handed the last artifact to a cheerful Vinca and the ever stoic Sorrel, who did his best to hide a slight smile. By that Friday Dula was up and about, announcing that they'd be having a party to celebrate the artifacts being returned to their rightful owners. The effect this had on the faeries was immediate, no one was calmly walking if they had the wings to fly, there was a constant chatter filled with giggles and smiling.

Geena took to sitting on the porch of the wizard hut after her morning run and basking in the magic that flowed through the fae land, Apatite. It amazed her that it was just as alive and full of life as the fae that lived there, that the two were so intertwined. Geena enjoyed the gleeful bliss until she found out that it wouldn't just be her wizard friends and the fae at this celebration.

"The fae leaders invited who?" Geena asked at dinner when the subject came up. Meda and Percy loved to live in blissful ignorance sometimes so they just looked adoringly at their full plates.

Mirzam finally answered, "Only the werewolves and vampires are coming but they invited the goblins, centaurs, and a few others."

"They don't think that werewolves and vampires in the same space is a bad idea?" Geena said before taking a bite of her steak.

"Anyone who comes has to sign an agreement when they enter, if they cause any trouble they are instantly teleported outside of Apatite, and the guards know not to let anyone back in," Mirzam answered calmly.

"They know that it will work?"

"I created it," Mirzam stated and that was enough to soothe Geena's worries. It was moments like this that reminded her she had not fully adjusted to not always having to be on guard. So used to everything being a threat, it was hard to just enjoy the slice of peace she enjoyed living among the fae and wizards.

A comfortable silence fell over the four of them as they simply enjoyed the food Percy had made. After a while Meda broke the silence, saying, "A faerie asked me to be their date to the celebration."

Always dramatic, Percy's silverware clattered to the floor. "What makes you think you can have a date, young lady?" The girls looked to see if he was just joking or if he had actually lost his mind.

"Young lady? I'm literally older than you," Meda scoffed.

"Only by two minutes."

"The best two minutes of my life." Meda's grip tightened around her steak knife. "Don't go playing the brother protector now, we both know you're late to that game."

"Don't go playing the brother protector now," Percy mocked Meda, dodging the spoon she threw at him. "Just a joke Andromeda," he insisted. "Anyway, who's the lucky girl?"

"Girl?" Geena blurted before thinking.

"Yeah. Men are not my thing. Women, however..." Meda stated flatly, looking to see if Geena would shun her.

Geena processed for barely a second before replying, "Oh that's cool, sometimes I feel behind with the three of you."

Mirzam laughed, nodding in agreement. "How do you think I feel with the two of them?" She gestured to the twins with her fork.

Standing up on his chair, Percy propped on foot on the table and declared, "No one can keep up with me."

Meda pushed his foot off, laughing when he lost his balance and jumped to the floor. "No one wants to. Her name is Lolium, works in the garden with the non-edible plants and isn't an asshole about wizards living here."

"When's the wedding?" Percy asked loudly, mumbling sorry when he remembered Mirzam had a headache.

"You wouldn't be invited if there was one," Meda snarled, obviously getting fed up with her brother. "Go to bed Perseus, before I turn you into a pancake."

As he sauntered out of the room, with the three girls giggling, he sang in a very high pitched voice, attempting to mimic an opera singer, "I LOOOOVE PANCAKEEEEEES."

The girls finished their meal in peace and after cleaning up, Mirzam brought Percy the rest of his food and told everyone they'd plan their outfits for the celebration after she got back from helping Vinca with inventory the next day.

CHAPTER ELEVEN:

Dula threw herself into setting up for the party—anything to continue avoiding Geena. It was almost a game of cat and mouse, Geena would work her way over to Dula to talk to her and tell her she's not angry with her, but Dula was off doing something else before Geena could even make it halfway to her. Geena tried to listen to Orrin when he told her to give it some time but she would catch Dula looking at her with her silver eyes drowning in sorrow and it haunted her.

It seemed all of the fairies needed the celebration to distract them from all of their hard work. Maintaining and protecting their land were their biggest priorities and the love and dedication that went into that was reflected in the party decorations.

Garlands of lavender and hydrangeas hung from every tree, firebirds donned a blueish tint to their flames rather than their signature striking red, and faeries were all around singing and hanging up more garlands or lights, adding to the majestic landscape. It reminded Geena of Christmas.

"GEENAAAA!" Percy sang as she walked up the steps to the market, propping his basket full of food on his head, freeing a hand for him to grab Geena's and place a light kiss on the back of hers.

"Hey stranger, need any help?" she asked and he shook his head in a reply. As he opened his mouth to say something a figure emerged from the drink area and stood in front of both of them.

"Geena, can I talk to you for a second?" Mortimer asked, ignoring Percy completely but not missing the slight movement he made that would block Mortimer for Geena to make an escape.

"It's alright," she said to Percy, "I'll see you back at the hut before the celebration." Percy lingered a second longer before continuing his shopping, but stayed within sight of Geena while she talked to Mortimer. Geena smiled at his lack of distance but appreciated that he trusted and listened to her.

"I just wanted to see how you were doing," Mortimer said. "I know you were with the healers for a couple days after your mission." He looked Geena over trying to see what would cause her to stay with the healer.

"Just some cuts and scrapes. Orrin wanted me to stay a little while longer just in case." She shrugged the question off ,adding, "He doesn't want to lose his daughter so soon after he got her back." She was not lying she told herself, she just wasn't telling him everything.

"I'm glad to see you are well." He hesitated a moment. "Maybe you can save me a dance at tonight's celebration?"

"I'll consider it," Geena said with finality, hoping to end the conversation. She turned to find Percy again and barely heard Mortimer say,

"I hope so."

————

The music had already begun by the time the wizards were finished getting ready. Meda was nervous and while she always looked put together her beauty was hypnotizing tonight. Geena admired her wild curly hair that twisted into an intricate design before cascading down her golden skin. Her cobalt blue dress covered in gold accents would have outshined anyone else's beauty but it only magnified Meda's.

"*Wow!*" Mirzam exclaimed. "Andromeda, you are a vision. Lolium won't know what to do other than pick her jaw up off of the ground." Meda blushed at the compliment before looking at Mirzam.

"Silver suits you, Mi'." Meda walked over to fix a few hairs that had escaped the end of Mirzam's braid. Mirzam's coils were partially tamed by the hair around her face braided and pinned back, leaving the rest of her hair natural and enchanting. Red pins secured her braids that matched her silver dress adorned with red gems.

"Both of you look amazing," Geena said. "I fear I pale in comparison." She stood and smoothed out her dress that she had borrowed from Orrin. He said that it was her mother's favorite, so he never got rid of it.

The dress was pure silk in a Tyrian purple that had an internal corset that accentuated Geena's waist, and she noticed her paranoid mother had modified the bodice to protect her internal organs from receiving any mortal damage. Other than golden gems around the neckline and hem, the royal color was alone in its magnificent display.

"Everyone decent?" Percy called from the other side of the door. "Lolium and Juniper are here." Mirzam opened the door to greet them.

"Hello Geena, I am Lolium. We have not officially met." Lolium approached offering her hand to shake, her ivory dress swished with her every move. Her green hair was the only pop of color in her ensemble. Geena shook her hand and let Meda tend to her date while she walked over to Juniper, Percy, and Mirzam.

"Don't all of you clean up nicely," Juniper offered, picking a piece of fuzz out of Percy's hair even as he swatted her away saying not to "mess with hard work." Juniper was in a red suit that complimented her. While the rest of them had complete outfits—even Percy had on a basic but classic black suit—Juniper opted to forgo shoes, though all of her nails were painted a striking black. Percy finally let his gaze fall onto Geena as she laughed at Juniper's comment. He froze in awe.

"Geena thinks she pales in comparison to us," Mirzam told the other two as Geena withered under Percy's undivided attention.

"Impossible," he muttered.

"I thought you were a poet, Perc." Juniper laid a hand on his shoulder, shaking him lightly. "You were quoting that one human poet earlier. What was the name again?"

Seeming to snap out of a daze, Percy began reciting a poem, *"There are taller than you, taller. / There are purer than you, purer. / There are lovelier than you, lovelier."* He paused for a moment before finishing, *"But you are the queen."*

"Pablo Neruda, good choice Percy," Mirzam supplied, "Though I doubt that is what you were quoting to Juni earlier."

"Whatever he quoted to me had something to do with a *Mistress eyes*," Juniper told Geena and Mirzam, realizing that the only thing Percy could add to the conversation was drool.

"Shakespeare's *My Mistress' Eyes* is not the sonnet to win over anyone, Percy!" Mirzam exclaimed.

"That's why he recited it to Juniper," Meda said as she finally rejoined the conversation. "Although smooth sailing with the *neurotic* person."

"*Neruda!*" Mirzam corrected.

"Shall we go? The music sounds lovely," Geena suggested, hoping no one would notice her cheeks matching her hair.

CHAPTER TWELVE:

The party's completed decor was of a magnitude that stunned Geena into a silence. She was mesmerized with the scenery, the music, everything. The attendees were just as beautiful as the decorations. It seemed everyone's attire fit into a mix between a royal ball and 1920s glamour. Dula had done an amazing job. Small explosions of fireworks continuously accented the empty areas in the sky and the music carried over the entire area even though the faeries playing stayed in the same spot in the middle of the expansive dance floor surrounded by dining tables.

"You look just as enchanting as your mother did in that dress," Sorrel offered as he approached.

"Oh," Geena put a hand over her heart to help calm its pace. She was slightly spooked at the compliment and the person it came from. "Thank you, Sorrel. You are quite the charmer tonight as well."

Sorrel smirked as a reply and gave her a drink. They stood beside each other taking in their surroundings as the song played its course and another song began. When Sorrel noticed Geena swaying along to the music, he finished the rest of his drink in one gulp and turned to her.

"Care to dance Geena Bellows?" Sorrel asked as he held out his arm. Geena looped her arm through his. "I promise not to purposely step on your toes. I'd hate to damage the second most beautiful person at this event." Geena looked at him, raising an eyebrow, wondering who was first. "Obviously," he said as they reached an empty space on the floor before turning to face her, "I am the first."

He placed his right hand along the middle of her back and began leading Geena with her hand in his left. Throughout the first verse, the pair remained quiet.

"Do you know what song this is?" Geena asked, removing her hand from his shoulder to fix some hair that had fallen in her eyes.

"*Baby, I'm Yours*, I believe," Sorrel responded, his blue hair shining in the light, the decor bringing out the different hues. "I'm sure the starting song selection is Vinca's, she's always preferred slower songs until she's had a few drinks,"

"What music does King Sorrel prefer?" Geena baited him with a teasing tone. She enjoyed his bewilderment at her addressing him formally.

"You don't have to... Sorrel is fine." He shook his head as he re-focused. "I'm not particularly picky when it comes to music."

"So you save all your pickiness for cobblers then?"

He laughed dryly as he *mistakenly* scuffed his shoe over hers, like he was about to step on her foot but stopped it at the last moment.

"Why are you being nice to me?" Geena blurted out, catching them both off guard, "You aren't exactly the same person who called me a half-breed and cut my hand up with thorns."

He looked down with a sigh and Geena could see his eyelashes were more purple than the blue of his hair.

"I shouldn't have done any of that, you just..." He stopped their dancing to grab two more drinks from a floating tray, handed one off to her and downed his in one go. "I was always cruel to your mother because she was different and I didn't understand her. I actually was quite fond of her by the time she got pregnant with you." He escorted Geena over to a table with some snacks and quickly made two small plates as he continued, "When she had to run away, I almost disposed of Cerise myself so she could stay. I may be the longest ruler of the five faerie leaders, but even I couldn't manage that without a rebellion."

Geena noticed Vinca making her way towards them, but she stopped at Sorrel holding his hand up and she simply waved and turned away.

"Then Mia was gone." Sorrel croaked, "Years later you show up and you look exactly like her. I can see her in you, with the way you move and even your actions sometimes. I didn't want to ruin the memories of Mia by trying to use you as a replacement."

Geena took their plates and set them down, holding one of his hands in hers. "Cruelty only brings more cruelty. Kindness is the only way to break the chaos."

He smiled sadly. "Mia used to say that." His voice was soft, and Geena had never seen Sorrel so *open*. There was always a fortified defense between him and everyone else. "A mutual friend reminded me of that saying, and that Mia would turn me into a blade of grass permanently if I attempted to treat you the same way I treated her for so long."

He took a breath and took Geena's hands in his. "I just want to apologize for my actions when you first got here. I can't promise I'll be nice, but I can promise that I'll never try to hurt you on purpose."

"Thank you." Geena meant it because one thing she valued over everything was the truth.

"Now go dance with your old man Orrin, he's been watching us like a hawk," Sorrel stated before he sauntered off with his usual arrogance, acting like he didn't have a sincere heart to heart with someone.

As Geena hugged Orrin and began speaking with him about what their days had been like, leaving out the Mortimer business, she noticed Vinca fixing Sorrel's hair before peppering his face with kisses. Geena laughed at the fact that he was far away from her and she could still see him blushing.

————

Dula stood on a platform wrapped up in a silver mesh dress that accentuated her wings and eyes. She took a swig from a bottle and cleared her throat before calling for attention, her voice clear for everyone to hear.

"Many of you are curious as to why this celebration has occurred tonight. We have some big news: the other week our wizard guests and myself went on a mission and we retrieved, not just one, but all three of the Artifacts of Fae back from The Score—the group of wizards who not only are after us and our talents, but other creatures as well, including those in attendance tonight."

Loud cheers reverberated through the air, so powerful that Geena felt it shake in her chest as the faeries, werewolves, and vampires in attendance roared with glee. The other wizards had joined Orrin and Geena soon before Dula's speech began, and not even they could contain their joy.

Dula's voice boomed over everyone else's, the potion she sipped doing its job. "So tonight they are our heroes! To those of you who are still unpleasant to the wizarding group, it will no longer be tolerated in any form after they have done something so important for us. So let this be the start of cordial alliances with others." Dula raised her arm, drink in hand with the biggest smile on her face, "Raise your glasses to peace and prosperity!"

The crowd echoed "Peace and prosperity!" Before the celebration resumed with tenfold the amount of emotion and excitement, Geena noted that Vinca's selection of slow songs must have finished as all of the music from that point on was upbeat and encouraged everyone to dance and celebrate. The wizards decided that they would not have a single care in the world and they celebrated more than anyone else. Geena was non-stop dancing by herself, with Percy, with Orrin, and she even managed to snag a dance from Lolium, which Meda pretended irritated her. The wizards did have to sit out of one intricate faerie dance but they were mesmerized as the faeries moved together gracefully like they were one live unit.

"Save a dance for me?" Mortimer approached Geena after everyone had been dancing for hours.

Wiping a few tears from her eyes from laughing at Mirzam and Percy dancing like chickens, she said, "I think I can manage one more as long as you play nice." She walked with him to an open area to dance.

The first minute or so they simply danced without talking. Geena could feel Mortimer's hand shaking in hers, so she decided she'd throw him a bone and break the silence, saying, "Have you enjoyed the party so far?"

"Yes I have. The music has been immaculate, along with the refreshments," Mortimer answered.

"So formal—you haven't had enough drinks to properly enjoy the night." Geena flipped some hair over her shoulder. "Any word with more than two or three syllables means you're not having a good time,"

"Is that so?" Mortimer countered, raising an eyebrow calling Geena's attention to his golden eyes.

"Duh," Geena said, like it was ridiculous Mortimer would have presumed differently.

"I notice one of mine is a date for one of yours." His face contorted in a way that seemed to shift the different shades of his skin around.

"Meda and Lolium have been laughing and having a good time all night long." She looked over them and smiled when she noticed that behind them Orrin was making animals made of water run around some faerie children. "I think they are cute."

"We have different definitions of cute," Mortimer mumbled and looked down when he noticed Geena picked up on what he said.

"You agreed to play nice," she reminded him. The song was coming to an end and Geena was grateful, not wanting anything to taint the good night she was having.

"Sorry," Mortimer offered. "How about a drink?" Geena agreed and followed him to a table with drinks. He fixed two flutes of a purple bubbling beverage and handed one to her.

"To peace and prosperity," she said, clinking her glass against his and taking a huge sip, not noticing that Mortimer hadn't drank any of his own yet.

She smiled at him, feeling giddy. A giggle bubbled out of her the same way the bubbles from bottom of her drink floated chaotically to the surface.

"Morty," Geena said, finally taking notice of his still full glass, "toast, drink."

He raised his glass to her, his golden eyes shifting to a darker tone. "To power and prosperity."

"That's not the toast," she slurred, suddenly feeling dizzy. She went to put a hand on his shoulder, but instead was enveloped by his presence. She shook her head to clear her blurry vision and shaky thoughts and was able to focus on his still full drink before she succumbed to whatever force pulled her under.

{ **13** }

CHAPTER THIRTEEN:

In the haze of partying, Percy was the first to notice something was off. Excusing himself from his friends, he made his way over to the best chance of an answer.

"Excuse me," Percy said, clearing his throat, "King Orrin." When he had Orrin's attention he asked, "Have you seen Geena?"

Orrin stood from where he had been playing with some faerie children. His pupils disappeared as he scanned the room, looking for her auburn hair or purple dress. His vision snapped back to Percy when did not find her.

"Are the rest of the wizards with you?" Orrin asked urgently. "Dula and Vinca are over there so she's not with them."

"They were. She went to dance with Mortimer the last I saw her." Percy followed Orrin towards Dula and Vinca. "Do you think she's alright?"

"To every higher power, I can only hope." Orrin put out the small fire show Vinca was doing to entertain herself and Dula, it sizzled with simply a wave of his hand. "Please tell me one of you knows where Geena is?"

While Vinca remained airy and light, Dula stood at attention immediately and quickly reached the same intensity as Orrin. Percy stayed a few steps behind, sensing the tension and not wanting to be a victim in any altercation.

"Who's on guard tonight? Is it Juniper?" Dula asked Orrin, who was usually in charge of guard schedules.

He nodded as he spoke. "She was here for the speech but she should now be posted at the east entrance as usual."

"Percy, can you get yourself and your crew dressed in something more suitable in case we have to leave to find Geena? Orrin and I will check in with Juniper," Dula ordered and waved Percy off.

"You don't think anything happened, do you?" Dula asked Orrin when it was just the two of them walking lightly toward the east entrance.

"I don't know what I think."

———

Geena's eyelids were heavy but her instincts were on overdrive when she finally emerged from her daze. She couldn't tell if she was about to vomit or pass out as she tugged on the chains attached to her wrists. Her head was spinning and she couldn't focus her vision on anything to stabilize herself. She stayed silent in hopes of gaining some indication of where she was. She knew she was out of Apatite; the air around her was heavy with chemicals and something dark. She was trying to place what it was, it was familiar and made her skin crawl, urging her to yank again on her chains, noticing she had matching ones on her feet as well. *No. No. No.* Geena hadn't been on the run in a little while but the instincts to get the hell out and feeling of dread kicked in all the same.

She tried to calm her breathing, not wanting to give in to the panic. The air was closing in on her, whatever put her in a daze was still in her system and fighting for control again. She whistled four quiet staccato notes and waited. When an orange blob broke through the fuzzy darkness, she waved her hand, concentrating on the little magic she could conjure, and whispered, "Get Orrin." The blob was gone and Geena's control was breaking under the daze again when she finally placed the feeling in the air.

It was *magic*, but dark, poisonous, twisted, and wrong wrong wrong.

—————

When Orrin and Dula broke through the door of the wizard hut with murder in their eyes and Juniper on their heels, Percy started grabbing weapons and attaching them to himself anywhere he could.

"She's gone," Orrin broke out, his demeanor cold and calculating but his voice was a stone balancing on a single toothpick.

"Mirzam, can you figure out a way we can find her? Track her?" Dula was a little more level headed, but her walls were cracking too.

Before Mirzam could answer, a firebird flew into the hut through an open window, swirling around until it was in front of Orrin. Geena's voice was small and shaky, but it was her voice that broke through the firebird, "Get Orrin."

"I can track that," Mirzam pointed at the bird and smiled at it when it landed on her finger. She took it to the kitchen island and was waving her wand around it trying to locate Geena while the rest began gathering weapons. Knowing Mirzam would be too hyper focused on tracking to think about weapons, he grabbed the ones she preferred to give her when she was done.

When they were all around the small dining table watching Mirzam all but dissect the firebird to get whatever information she could for minutes, she lifted her head and made eye contact with Meda and Percy. Her eyes were sad when she finally said, "Cepheus."

—————

When Geena broke free of the daze the second time, the feeling of dark magic was even stronger but her surroundings weren't as isolated, people were around her. Her hearing would go in and out but she would never miss one name, one she had heard in fear, in anger, one she had heard for years, the name she had been running from, the name that is the reason her mom is dead... *Cepheus*.

The name that finally Geena used to finally pull her out of the daze completely, Cepheus stood in front of her, looming over her as she realized she was chained to a chair. His smile held no warmth, a chill was the warmest this smile could be. His hair was pepper with salt sprinkled in and eyes she knew, soft green eyes that were always friendly, the eyes looked wrong on him... when the pieces finally snapped together it felt like being stabbed.

"The Score?" Geena looked to Percy. "Like the mafia that has been trying to kill me?"

Meda responded, "Yes and also the mafia that," she pointed out between her and Percy, "our Dad is the leader of."

Geena felt for her magic but couldn't grasp it, so with her hands and feet chained to her chair she did the only thing she could think of. She spit in his face.

"You half-breed bitch," Cepheus yelled and that's when Geena noticed that her aim was better than she thought. "She fucking spit in my eye," he yelled at the others who were moving forward to help their leader.

"Hello Cepheus," Geena thanked Circe that her voice was level as she greeted the mountain of muscle that had hunted the entire continent for her.

"Fuck you Bellows," he spit as his fist connected with her. Geena couldn't tell if it was the punch or the impact of her head meeting the stone floor, but she faded again.

————

Vinca could sense that something was off. She had enjoyed the party but something still pushed her off-kilter. On a whim, she decided to check on the artifacts. Even the Faerie Queen of fire needed her burns soothed, and the sting of the artifacts being stolen was as fresh as ever, only setting her eyes upon them could pacify her.

Vinca nodded to the guards who were outside of the Council room as they opened the door for her. Expecting to greet the guard inside, she was met with a hollow room. There was nothing displayed behind the thrones... they were gone. The artifacts that had just been returned were gone.

———

"What's the plan?" Dula asked Mirzam as their group stood a little ways from the building Mirzam had tracked the firebird too, a building that the three wizards looked at with discomfort and disgust.

"Get Geena and get out. The only element of pure surprise that we have is that Perseus, Andromeda, and myself are supposed to be dead. Cepheus isn't arrogant enough to believe that someone wouldn't notice Geena missing from the fae by now." Mirzam's hands were shaking as she gathered her hair and secured it with a clip. "Wait... are the artifacts still in Apatite? Who was in charge of guarding them tonight?"

Orrin may have been King of Water, but he could have produced fire with his stare. "Mortimer. Mortimer was one of the guards but Percy said he was dancing with Geena."

"Shit," Meda said, "Would Mortimer take her?"

"If he did, he's dead." Orrin was vibrating with fury. "I'll fill him up with liquid until he explodes out of his skin."

Dula put an arm on Orrin to steady his rage and she pulled some half-assed plan out of thin air. Once the wizards got everyone into the building, they were to fall back and follow behind the two fae leaders watching their backs and staying hidden.

"And when we find Geena?" Percy asked.

"Grab her, get out, grab the artifacts if you can, but Geena is the priority," Dula answered.

"I do not mean to overstep, Queen Dula, but will you be okay to go in so soon after the chest incident?" Andromeda asked sheepishly.

"I appreciate your concern Andromeda, but consider this my apology to Geena while simultaneously getting revenge on those filthy wizards that did that."

A firebird that barely contained any orange glow flew to Dula with a note.

The Artifacts of Fae are missing.

- *Vinca*

––––––

Geena opened her eyes to a myriad of candles set around her. Her chains were now bolted to the floor, spreading her limbs like a starfish. Craning her neck she saw the Artifacts of Fae behind her, and looking around the rest of the room she could manage to see, she saw Mortimer.

"Morty," she said, pulling at the chains, "help me out of these." When another person stepped out of the shadows, Geena frowned.

"He won't be doing that, *mutt*," the girl spit out the last word, looking like a copy and paste of Cepheus with feminine features. "That faerie is working for my dad, who you might have met." The girl pulled out a knife and tilted Geena's chin to the side with it. "You've at least met his right hook. I didn't know we were planning to tenderize the meat before we cook it."

"Eris, get away from the half-breed," Cepheus' voice echoed off of the walls as his footsteps got closer. "We're about to begin, take some of her blood."

Eris procured multiple vials and used her knife to cut Geena's arms and collect her blood weeping from the wound. She smiled at Geena's discomfort.

"At least one of my children isn't a huge disappointment," Cepheus remarked to a woman against the wall where Geena couldn't see but she heard the reply the woman gave.

"We did well with Eris, darling." Her voice was smooth like filtered honey.

"That we did, Pandora." Geena imagined he spoke with as much love as he could, but it didn't sound much different than when he was spitting venom at her. "That we did."

{ **14** }

CHAPTER FOURTEEN:

Their entrance to the building was smoother than expected, but that did nothing to settle their nerves. Mirzam told them that getting through the guarding spells was easy, considering she made them. Percy was struggling more than the other two wizards with being back from where they had escaped. When they retrieved the artifacts, he was focused and calm. With Geena missing, he was terrified and couldn't stay focused on anything except his worries. Meda stopped once or twice to remind Percy to take a few deep breaths in order to calm his growing anxiety. It was a rare moment of calm kindness between the two that made Mirzam smile sadly—she had forgotten how much harder living here had been for Percy compared to the two of them, and forgotten the multitude of times Percy took the blame for any missteps that he did and didn't commit.

"Do you know where they might have her?" Orrin whispered to Mirzam as they ventured through the hallways of the building.

"Maybe the chamber? Cepheus always did his important meetings or *torturing* there," she replied and the whole group shuddered at what they feared Geena might be enduring. "I'll lead the way, if you don't mind?"

Orrin gestured for her to lead and followed her with the others. They had navigated up to the third floor and through the maze of hallways which Meda said were designed that way to make it harder for outsiders to get in or out, when they heard voices. Percy inhaled sharply through his nose. Meda whispered, "That's the room."

There were five visible wizards outside of the door to the room, but there were five of them too. Regardless of what Sorrel always said, the wizards were proficient in hand-to-hand combat, so if it came to that Orrin was not worried. He was about to suggest everyone pick a person to take down quietly, when Mirzam showed him an apple shaped device.

She pointed at the device, then to the guards, saying, "Sleep for at least three hours." Orrin grinned at her genius.

"What about us?" Dula hissed quietly.

Mirzam then produced a small square from her pocket which was switched to "off" and pointed at the "on" side. That was her answer. In the back of Orrin's mind he wanted to ask her all the details of this device, but the forefront stayed the same and it was the utter urgency to get Geena out, keep her alive. Dula nodded at Mirzam and gestured for her to go ahead.

The device landed with a muted thump in front of the wizards after she threw it at them. Mirzam couldn't hide her smile as they circled around the seemingly harmless object to investigate. She flipped the switch and a soft *psssss* sound was made as a silver mist came out of the device like smoke from a dying fire. Before the guards could make any sound, they were dropping to the floor, eyes rolled back. Meda and Percy cast charms that silenced their falls as Mirzam cut off the device. She looked at Dula and shrugged with a look that said *See? That wasn't so bad.*

———

Geena winced as Eris rubbed a mixture of salt and sand into the cut she had taken blood from earlier. Eris, who she figured to be Meda and Percy's sister, held none of their features, her eyes were the color of burnt orange and full of mirth as she caused Geena pain. Where the twins were light and friendly, Eris was dark and violent.

Cepheus was emptying the vials of her blood into a bowl that already contained the salt and sand mixture. When the last vial was emptied, he swiftly pricked his own finger and added a drop or two, mixing his blood with hers.

"Put the artifacts in place, Eris," he ordered. "Those vile things will notice her absence soon."

Geena tried to speak but had to cough to find her voice. "Why are you doing this? Why me?"

"Pandora, draw a circle with this blood around her then give me the bowl back," Cepheus ordered, before he grabbed a long sword off of the wall that Geena had noticed earlier and hoped was for decoration. "Well, those faerie shits are a waste of magical properties."

Geena sputtered to defend them but Cepheus talked over her.

"Fae are nothing except demoted angels and demons too weak to cause havoc. We were at war, killing them until their numbers had dwindled significantly." Cepheus smiled softly. "That is, until too many other creatures were caught in the crossfire and their leaders came together and signed that damn treaty."

"The one that stopped the constant fighting between us?" Geena questioned.

"Yes, that disgraceful thing. The other rules I could understand. *Don't out others to humans. Don't reveal yourself to humans. Don't steal from the dragon banks,*" he said mockingly. "But cease all wars for all magical peoples to recover their populations? The wizards are the only ones smart enough to not be endangered, but that didn't stop some idiotic wizards from signing that damn bill."

Pandora had finished the blood circle surrounding Geena and gave the bowl back to Cepheus. He nodded at her and she returned to her place by the wall. Eris had set the cup artifact between Geena's chained legs, the chest at her left side, and the scroll at her right. Without so much of her magic available, Geena could see what the artifacts truly were. The cup was a book, as she had guessed previously. The chest was a crystal of some kind and the scroll was a stick—*No. It was a wand.* Geena hid her confusion from sight as Cepheus continued.

"Now, hopefully you're smart enough to understand why I'm doing this," he said as he approached her. "I found out about the artifacts and realized I could steal all of those faerie powers and make them obey me."

"So make them your slaves?" She spit at him, her voice dripping in disgust.

He shrugged as he dipped his fingertips in the bowl of blood. "Call it whatever you want." He flicked the blood onto the *cup* before making his way to the *chest* and doing the same thing. "The trouble was finding the missing piece," he said as flicked blood over the *scroll*, "finding a half-breed. A wizard and faerie mixture." He set the bowl down and gestured to Geena. "That's where you come in. Now the faeries don't often mingle with those outside of their own, but they never interacted with wizards in a peaceful manner until Mia."

Geena flinched at her mother's name, and her gut twisted in disgust when she realized the name fell off of his lips with familiarity. "You knew my mom?"

Cepheus laughed and crouched beside her, "Knew her? We were engaged."

{ **15** }

CHAPTER FIFTEEN:

Geena looked at Cepheus, disgusted, wondering if he was lying and then wondering if it was true, what her mother could have seen in his cold eyes.

"Mia dumped me after we had the same fight about six times, that she shouldn't be friends with any faeries, let alone one with hideously huge horns." His voice was laced with venom. "I got over her, but the sting of a faerie being chosen over a wizard does not go away. It festers and spreads. I made a family of my own and set about to find a way to not just destroy the faerie that was chosen over me, but to destroy them all."

"You're fucking insane," Geena stated. Eris made a noise of contempt and started to lunge toward Geena but was stopped at Cepheus holding up his hand.

"The answer to all of my problems came to me one Christmas. My Pandora and I were taking our eldest two out to look at lights and decorations humans put up. It was the only thing Pandora and I liked that humans did, when I saw a familiar figure and an almost miniature version beside her." Cepheus pointed at Geena. "It was Mia and a little Mia except the little one's hair would glow with excitement at the decorations. A wizard's hair doesn't glow, it might spark in anger, but that's rare. It wasn't hard to put the pieces together that Mia had become brainwashed enough to reproduce with a faerie considering how she defended them as her friends."

Cepheus reached into the bowl again and gathered some blood to spread over Geena's forehead before pouring what was left over her chest. "Since you are part wizard, doing this ritual with you binds the faeries to a wizard. If you were half vampire, the ritual would bind the fae to them." Cepheus stood and went over to the table that Eris hovered next to beside Mortimer.

"You're okay with being a slave?" Geena asked Mortimer.

"I won't be a part of that. Cepheus said he found a way to exclude me for my services to him. The faeries that never saw my true potential and walked all over me will pay and I walk away free." Mortimer's golden eyes glowed, "I was promised power and I intend to collect," he said, the candlelight adding more dimension to his multi-colored skin as he puffed his chest out and smiled triumphantly.

"I do have a way to exclude you from that," Cepheus said with a devious grin. "Would you take care of that, Eris?"

"Of course, Father." Eris smiled like a Cheshire cat and barely seemed to move. The sight of Mortimer's head rolling toward Geena registered before the sound of the blade that Eris had used whipped through the air. "His eyes will make nice decor, don't you think?" she asked as she threaded her fingers in Mortimer's hair and held his head up to Cepheus.

Geena turned away in horror, meeting Pandora's eyes and seeing that she was just as horrified with the display. Pandora hid her expression, with a speed that conveyed practice, under a blank slate of a face before Cepheus spoke, "Now with the faerie sacrifice, we can begin."

————

Geena felt magic rolling over her in waves as Cepheus began the ritual spells. She had little to no magic of her own available and the second she thought she had a grip on anything, it would slip away. It was like trying to start a fire in the rain. As Cepheus rattled off spell after spell, the heat of his dark magic drained her own magic like a sauna would sweat. The feeling of her magic being taken from her made her feel how damp the air was, whether from the magic or her sweating in efforts to break free. she could almost grasp at the individual droplets of water in the air that were contributing to the humidity.

He walked to the circle and placed a foot on each side of her. Cepheus stood tall and confident with the giant sword in his hands, the blade pointed at the blood-soaked section of her chest. The rhythmic chanting continued as the point of the blade descended slowly. She kept her eyes open, determined that even if she didn't survive this, she would haunt Cepheus into madness by making him replay the light fading from her eyes. He would see her in every watery reflection.

"It's a downright shame. I do hate spilling wizard blood, even tainted as yours is," Cepheus raised the tip of the blade from where it had made an indention in her dress, building momentum to bring the blade back down. Geena supposed things could be worse, slower, more painful than this death approaching her.

A flash of light registered before Geena recognized the scent of rain, fresh rain, inside of a closed room, water, *water*. Dula stood over her, a smirk settled on her face as she ripped through the chains like they were nothing but paper. Without giving her much time to realize that maybe she wasn't going to die tonight, Dula cut Geena's floor length dress to now fall below her knees and shoved a sword in her hands. Spells were flying all around, bouncing off the walls, as everything started coming into focus. Geena's instincts took over—she had been fighting so long that it was as easy as breathing, so she did not hesitate to drop to the floor as magical fire strained through the air where her head was. Drawn to the flying water, Geena gravitated to it. Spinning and making her way to where Orrin was handling both Cepheus and Eris, she almost missed the spells that were flying through the doorway, their casters not visible, and she realized that her wizard friends were here too. The rest of her family was here.

A gargantuan thud paused everyone's movements, as a brick object laid in the middle of the room, almost in the center of the blood circle Geena had been chained into.

"Fight like we train," Mirzam's voice was loud and clear, and Geena saw the recognition and anger flash over Cepheus' face as the brick exploded into a light blue powder that covered the room. Eris went to cast a spell, waving her wand in a grand gesture as she screamed her spell in anger. When not even a faint color appeared, Geena charged with a sword, gaining Eris' undivided attention as she dodged the attack. Orrin focused his efforts solely on Cepheus, attacking with a passion and ruthlessness that few people can achieve. When Geena dodged a flying fist, she caught sight of Dula putting the artifacts in a bag. Eris must've noticed as well as she directed her war path to Dula, forgetting her current opponent.

It happened so fast, Geena couldn't even warn Dula of the blade that flew through the air as it left Eris' extended hand. When Geena managed to scream Dula's name, she was already feet away, another figure stood in her place.

"Perseus!" Geena stood frozen and the voice reverberated through the room. She took note of the blade's placement, too high to be the heart, but muscles would take weeks to heal even with magic. "Stop! Stop! Stop!" the voice screeched like a banshee's warning.

"My son, my boy," Pandora stood in front of Perseus, running her hands over his face, through his hair as if she had moments to memorize the feel of him before he vanished from sight.

"Hi Momma." Percy's voice was strained, quiet. He didn't hesitate to slam whatever was in his left hand into Pandora's side; however, he simply caught as much of her weight as he could with one arm as Pandora's lost consciousness. Meda was suddenly there to support the weight Percy couldn't manage.

With Percy injured, Dula and Orrin fighting off Cepheus, and Eris who fought like demons even without their magic, Geena began to panic. She felt something like anxiety build through her starting at her stomach and bubbling up to her heart. It almost felt like it was raining in the room. Mirzam and Meda were occupied and so they couldn't help when Orrin and Dula began to fall back, taking blows that were tearing them down. Geena couldn't tell if her heart was racing to its death or if it had already stopped, but the explosion didn't surprise her. She saw the sword that Cepheus had placed over her heart soar through the air and Geena felt all of the air leave her body. She had lost her mother, could not do anything to save her, she would not lose her father too. Seeing the blade racing towards Orrin, something inside of her snapped and the explosion came right after.

Her feet were planted on the ground and she was surrounded by water. It only took a moment for Geena to realize that Dula and Orrin were just as incapable of using their magic as the wizards were.

The water licked Geena's skin clean, healing her from the inside out. She felt like she was fresh, new, with something she didn't have before... *power.* She commanded the water fall away from her family, and it listened, she commanded the water push Cepheus and Eris out of the room and into the hallway, *and it listened.*

Whatever dormant faerie part of her that she tried to reach when attempting potion after potion with Dula, it was awake now and it had arrived with a vengeance.

She grabbed the bag of artifacts that Dula had dropped when Percy pushed her out of the way of the blade and walked over to the two faerie leaders, the water parting around Geena as she made her way to where they were standing in a bubble, water not touching them but surrounding them. The two fae could do nothing but robotically follow her in their shock. She collected them and made her way to the only other bubble, where Percy was crouched holding a shaking hand over his wound and Meda and Mirzam held onto Pandora's sleeping form. Meda's fingers were white with the grip she had on her mother's arm.

"What happened?" Meda asked, her wet hair stuck to her neck and shoulders.

"How many of you still have on the bracelets Mirzam made us for the mission?" Geena asked, pointing at her wrist, hating herself for not thinking of the bracelet sooner. Mirzam and Meda held up their wrists, showcasing the matching bracelets when Dula shook hers. "Dula, take Percy. Mirzam and Meda, I trust you'll handle her," Geena gestured to Pandora, and was met with their nods. "I got Orrin. Then we'll lick our wounds, I'll explain what happened with me and then we…"

Orrin finished her sentence when she faded off, "figure out what to do with the mother and then plan our next moves."

The group all nodded, all of their eyes were sparkling in shock and exhaustion. While everyone's shock had a different origin, whether near-death, loss, pain, family, the exhaustion was easy to notice and one they all shared.

"Ready?" Geena asked as everyone paired off and got their bracelets ready. She hooked a bloodied arm through Orrin's, wincing when remaining salt and sand rubbed against her cut, and tapped the bracelet three times. She had blinked and missed the room dissolve into the woods by an entrance to the fae land. A faerie was hovering over the ground with a hand on their chest, obviously spooked by the sudden appearances, but quickly relaxed and smiled as the group popped into existence.

"You're all alive!" Juniper said. "Geena, we have to stop meeting with you looking like absolute shit," she tried to joke but the crowd was tough, which didn't bother Juniper as she continued, "It hurts my eyes to have to see messed up things."

{ **16** }

CHAPTER SIXTEEN:

Geena had the least amount of damage considering how close she was to her death. The healers quickly dismissed her after stitching up her few cuts and demanded she refrain from using any magic in the next few days as her magical core had been weakened from whatever suppressed her magic and then the explosion. She quickly found a way to keep herself busy as she didn't want to be left with her thoughts just yet. The only person who wasn't still being tended to by the healers was Pandora, who sat in a locked room, with her wand stowed away elsewhere. This wasn't Geena's smartest idea, but she didn't know what else to do and she didn't want to be alone either.

The door creaked as Geena shut it behind her and approached the figure that was sitting up in a basic cot, barren except for a flimsy white blanket. Pandora did not say anything as Geena pulled up a chair and sat towards the end of the cot, but she watched Geena, eyes trained on her like a hawk waiting for any wrong movement, either to escape or attack.

"It's quite uncanny," Pandora said as she began pulling her furiously coily hair into a bun that showcased her two gray streaks on either side of her head, "your resemblance to your mother, Mia. I wasn't close with her, but she was always hypnotic in her kindness."

"I didn't realize you knew her," Geena mumbled, not sure if she wanted to stay to hear what Pandora might say, but she remained in her seat, not willing to give up the chance to eat up more information on her mother.

"We were in the same tutoring group—that is the way wizards usually learn how to control their magic, schools were always too big and too much of a risk since they attract attention, though there were some." Pandora was stiff but her eyes were tired. "My children, are they alright? No one has told me anything."

"Meda's fine, she's helping tend to Percy who will be okay once they control the blood flow." Geena saw the concern expand in Pandora's eyes. "Your other lovely child had the knife dipped in venom, but they are countering its effects."

Pandora's composure shattered like glass, her sobs warped her body as she mumbled the twins' names. "Andromeda and Perseus are alive," she choked out as if the realization was finally setting in. "I sifted through every piece of ash for them when that building exploded. I mourned them, missed them, and loved them so much. More than anything I was happy they escaped Cepheus, he was never kind to them, especially Percy. He would always take the blame for things Andromeda or Mirzam did. Said I ruined them before they were even three and demanded a child that wasn't soft; he said if a child was going to be malleable then it should be made a weapon, not a weakness. I missed them every day, but I envied them every moment that they had escaped."

Pandora, who clearly had years of practice in controlling her expression, was visibly struggling under Geena's gaze.

"Now I can get them back or at least they are alive." Pandora laughed without any humor before sobbing again, "they are alive and as long as they are happy, I will survive."

Geena stood and tentatively took Pandora's hand, "Meda likes to work in the gardens here. She usually comes home with dirt all over her work clothes but not a single speck is on her, nor a single hair out of her braid." Pandora smiled as tears fell down her cheeks, "Percy cooks for all of us, one of the faerie leaders is quite fond of his blackberry cobblers too. He spends the rest of his time annoying either Meda, Mirzam, or myself. If he is going to sing as much as he does, he needs to consider some lessons."

When Pandora broke into uncontrollable sobs that shook the cot, Geena engulfed her in a hug and could barely make out what Pandora mumbled over and over into Geena's hair. *I'm sorry.*

———

Geena ambled through the trees outside of the healer hut when she saw a flash of blond hair. Before Geena could register anything else she was enveloped in a hug that could've kept her together if she was falling apart.

"You're okay, right? You're alright?" Orrin finally pulled away after a few long moments of just holding her, his eyes scanning over her for anything healer might have missed. Geena just smiled up at him and nodded before going for another hug that both of them seemed to need in order to keep going. Holding each other together so they wouldn't fall apart.

"Hey Geena, Orrin," they turned to see Juniper outside of the door of the healer hut, waving them over with a smile on her face. "Percy's awake, he's asking for the two of you."

The walk to Percy's room took less than a minute, but Geena's body felt like it had been running for hours, and her wrists ached. The fae healers gave her a paste to put on her wrists once a day but the chains were so tight that Geena still felt the weight of them now. When they walked into Percy's room, he was sitting up on a much nicer bed than Geena had found Pandora in and was eating something out of a bowl.

"Room service here is awful," Percy said as he continued to shovel food in his mouth. "Also is the food supposed to keep people here or make sure they never come back?" Even with his complaints, it did not stop him from finishing his bowl quickly.

"How are you feeling?" Geena asked and gestured to his bandaged right shoulder.

"Like a blade made love to my collarbone," Percy replied with such a straight face, but his eyes gave away his joking nature.

"So, you're feeling alright then. Good." Geena looked around and noticed that Mirzam and Meda were already here, but no Dula. "What do we do now? We need to figure it out soon, especially since I have about thirty minutes in me before I crash and sleep for at least twelve hours."

"You can't sleep for twelve hours," Meda challenged, raising her eyebrows at Geena.

"Well, I will now just to prove it to you."

"What's going to happen to Mom?" Percy blurted out.

Everyone slowly looked to Orrin, who didn't seem confident in his posture. "She can't stay here. The Council would never grant her refuge here like we did with the three of you. She didn't escape on her own, we took her."

"She hated it there! She hated him! She can help us, because no matter how independent my dumbass father is, he always needed someone to pat him on the back and tell him how good he was at what he was doing, and that's what he used my Mom for. She won't know everything, but she can help!" Geena had never seen Percy anything but giddy and joking or mellow at best, but the passion was pouring out of him, his jugular distinct as he yelled in defense of his mom.

"I'm sorry Percy, I really am," Orrin said. "You can still take it to the Council, but I'm telling you there is no argument that would convince the other faeries."

"I think I should leave Apatite," Geena spoke quietly but everyone froze at her words. Before they could rebut her idea she continued, "Cepheus will keep coming for me, he needs me for the ritual he was trying to do. It would drain the power from not only this land but the faeries themselves and with me being half fae and half wizard, it would bind the fae to the wizards, specifically Cepheus."

"That's why he was chasing after you?" Meda asked.

"Yes, and he found a way to get to me even from within here. He had Mortimer on his side, who else might be working with him?" The door opened, but Geena continued, "He will use another fae to get to me somehow. I can't stay here and put you all at risk. I was on the run for years; I can do it again."

"She's right." Pandora stood beside Dula with her hands cuffed in front of her. "I don't know names or anything to identify them, but that boy wasn't the only one that Cepheus had been conspiring with."

The twins were in shock at the sight of their mother, standing tall, hair perfectly in place, handcuffed but still managing to keep the facade of icy indifference on her face.

"I can take your mom with me too. That solves most of the problems," Geena said as she took a seat across from Mirzam at the foot of Percy's bed.

"No." Orrin didn't say anything else, but it was clear that his reply was to many things.

"It's not safe for any of us to stay here," Mirzam began, wringing her hands as she shuffled through all of the information she knew before continuing, "Geena can't stay for her reasons, Meda and Percy can't stay because Cepheus knows they are alive now, Orrin can't stay because any fae will be able to tell Cepheus that he's Geena father, I can't stay because I can be used to lure any of you out." She gestured to the twins and Geena. "I think Dula is the only one who can manage to stay but we may have to cause a scene for everyone to believe it."

"I don't think I'm the first half fae/half wizard," Geena said. Dula and Orrin looked the most confused, but Geena continued, "The artifacts—I was able to see what they truly were after my magic had been gone for so long, the scroll... it isn't a scroll."

"Geena, honey," Dula said, "it is a scroll. It's the only artifact that doesn't have the protective magic that changes its appearance."

"It's not a scroll."

"What is it? If it's not a scroll?" Orrin asked, trying his best to understand, but his tone betrayed his annoyance.

"It's a wand. There has to be a reason that only I can see the scroll as a wand, and why is it a wand if it wasn't made by someone like me? I need to find them," Geena explained.

Everyone was deep in thought for a few moments before Orrin broke the silence.

"Holy shit," he whispered, "I thought it was a dumb myth, a joke, but maybe it isn't."

"What are you talking about?" Dula asked.

"Mia had this book, I don't know where it is now, but it had this story in it about a wizard who wasn't fully a wizard but no one could ever figure out what the wizard truly was. It was just called The Old One in the story but now that I think about it, it had a lot of fae characteristics." Orrin started pacing as he relayed the information.

"So we are going to believe a story?" Dula asked as she looked at Orrin as if he sprouted additional horns on his shoulders.

"What else is there for us to do?" Orrin supplied.

The group was quiet for minutes, soaking in whatever plan was getting ready to be made and how it would change what they knew as their home.

"Mirzam, Meda, make us a list of everything we might need with us on the run. Percy... just focus on getting better and resting, we can't afford to be as vulnerable when we leave. Orrin, will you help me figure out something that can cause a convincing enough scene to be able to leave Dula behind?" Geena continued when he gave her a simple nod, "Dula, can you see if you can find out if anyone is acting weird? Outside of us, only Juniper knew that I was gone right?"

Dula confirmed that Juniper and maybe Vinca were the only ones who would know and that was when Meda and Mirzam made their way to the door, Meda stopping to kiss Pandora on the cheek before leaving.

"What about me?" Pandora asked when Dula followed the girls out, leaving the key to her cuffs with Orrin.

"Don't betray us. I don't trust you, but I trust Percy and Meda," Orrin said. "However if you betray us, I will make sure the twins don't see it, but I will waterboard you until I have felt like you have suffered enough and then I will take every molecule of water out of your body and leave you as dry as a dead leaf."

"Fair enough. Can I sit with my boy now?" Pandora said, unfazed by the threat.

CHAPTER SEVENTEEN:

"You dastardly bitch!" Dula screeched. The air was thick and sticky as she marched toward Geena. "Tried to steal MY POWERS and leave me like a fish out of water!"

The best lies are always dripping in truth.

"You have no proof." Geena paled at the feral glimmer in Dula's silver eyes. The last time she saw Dula's eyes look like that, she was trying to kill Geena.

"Couldn't take it could you? Wanted to be a part of something so much, wanted to fit in with a family you could never have." Dula was approaching with the smooth movements of a snake, venomous and on the hunt.

Geena didn't have enough time to continue her verbal "defense" against Dula so she did what she thought would be the only thing to finalize the betrayal. She shot a spell at her. With her wand gone, thanks to Mortimer taking it, she couldn't concentrate her magic enough to continuously produce powerful spells, so she kept to mostly slight annoyances, a sting, an itch.

Dula replied with assaults of water that stung as the pressure behind them was great enough for Geena to not have to fake her grunts of discomfort.

A crowd had formed around them, everyone was frozen in shock at the scene. Lolium had been one of the first to arrive since Dula and Geena had decided that near the gardens was the best place to act out their plan. Geena's heart sank as she remembered that Andromeda would be leaving, and wasn't able to even tell Lolium good-bye.

Most of Geena's spells were sparks of light for show and required little energy but she was running on steam and she needed to reserve her magic for her final blow. It was Dula's idea. She had found Orrin and Geena and told them of her plan. They couldn't think of anything better so they agreed and Orrin prepared his own and Geena's stuff before leaving with the twins, Pandora, and Mirzam.

Geena met Dula's icy stare and the fae queen managed a slight nod, telling Geena that it was okay. While jumping over and rolling out of the way of jets of water, Geena formed a ball of magic between her hands and before anyone could stop her, she shot it at Dula. The orange ball met Dula's chest and knocked her to the ground with a resounding thud. The water that Dula had been controlling fell to the ground; she didn't move from where she landed. As the faeries began to move toward Geena she tapped her bracelet three times and escaped.

———

Geena was unable to catch herself as she landed, and she barely managed not to get a face full of dirt that was turning into mud at a rapid pace as the weather outside of Apatite was borderline torrential. She quickly stood up and pulled herself together before making her way towards where some of her friends should be waiting for her. Without a wand to help concentrate and control her magic, Geena worried for Dula and hoped the spell didn't harm her, just make her sleep for a few hours, but there was no way to tell.

She hoped she didn't run into anyone from the Score. She knew she did not have the strength to protect herself by spells alone and the idea of manipulating water like she did at their headquarters made her dizzy with confusion. Geena did not know how she did it and she hadn't had time to catch on any of the many things running through her mind.

"*Psst*," a voice broke through the patch of trees to her left. "Geena?"

"Mirzam? Is that you?" Geena was on guard as much as she could be through a tired haze.

"Yeah, come on," Mirzam said as she approached and Geena only relaxed when she saw the matching bracelet on her wrist. "The others are at this small inn on the edge of a town a few miles away. We are staying there for the night and leaving in the morning."

"Isn't that a little close to stop?" Geena asked, taking Mirzam's arm when it was offered to help her make her way over a fallen tree.

"They'll be expecting us to get as far away as we can," Mirzam said, her voice light as usual, "and we'll be right under their nose."

"You're too smart for your own good."

Geena was met with Mirzam's giggle before she spoke, "Good."

———

The inn where they were staying was rickety and did not even have a sign outside. It was not clear that it was an inn until you were right at the front door, where there was a piece of paper yellowed with age that had "Pickle's Inn" written on it alongside a crayon drawing of a pig. The bell rang out Geena's and Mirzam's entrance.

"Welcome to Pickle's Inn, we sell homemade pickles and a place to..." the man behind the desk began in a practiced and monotone voice, before he looked up. "Oh, it's you."

He waved them off, mumbling about the mud they tracked in. Geena wouldn't have thought this place was operational from the outside but inside was clearly habitable, though it lacked the homey comfort of the wizard hut.

Mirzam led Geena to their room and opened the door with her key and Geena was shocked to see the whole crew inside. The size and number of beds in one wide room shocked Geena more than the fact that Meda and Percy were yelling about something while Orrin was perched on the top of bunk beds plugging his ears. Pandora was simply sitting in a chair in the corner, her expression unfazed by the chaos.

"I can't believe you didn't pack my favorite pillow, Meda!" Percy shouted.

"You could've gotten it yourself,"

"I was with the healers fixing my... oh hey Geena," Percy said. "You made it out!"

Orrin was off of his bed and checking over Geena before enveloping her in a hug. When Orrin finally released her, Meda was next to welcome back Geena.

"I would also hug you, but you know," Percy said, pointing at his right arm that was in a sling.

"Alright guys, we need to go to sleep soon, have we used enough magic to make a bed for everyone?" Mirzam announced getting them back on track for their mission. "We have a lot of ground to cover tomorrow."

{ 18 }

CHAPTER EIGHTEEN:

"Would it be too risky to try and stay in another fae land?" Mirzam asked Orrin as the group was treading through the trees not far from a main road that they were following to the next town.

Orrin was looking over a map when he pointed out a spot by a waterway. "The Hematite fae land is in between this collection of streams, they are one of the friendliest of the remaining fae clans. They might let us stay with them for a day or two, but any longer would be extremely risky. They do have an outer-layer of their land that is for their non-fae allies; I don't think it's a bad idea."

"Are they friendly with wizards though?" Mirzam asked, looking at the map.

"To those with good intentions, yes."

"It'll take a few days to get there, maybe a week with Percy and Geena as worn out as they are," Mirzam pointed out.

"Are we opposed to a little theft?" Pandora's voice was quiet but firm as she walked faster to be in line with Mirzam and Orrin.

"Depends on what would be stolen," Orrin said, raising his eyebrows at her suggestion.

"Just a car, more likely a van or SUV for all of us. We'll move faster and it helps us keep moving until everyone is recovered."

"I can jump start a vehicle," Mirzam stated. "As long as everyone else agrees, I think it's a good idea."

"Do you know how to drive a car?"

"Yeah, they're quite common for wizards to use these days," Mirzam answered Orrin.

Orrin looked to the other three who were listening but hadn't said anything yet. He was tired and he had not done as much as they had, especially Geena and Percy, who looked seconds away from collapsing.

"Let's steal a car then."

———————

Dula opened her eyes to people surrounding her and a bright light above where she was laying.

"Oh thank goodness, you're awake," Vinca cried as she clasped Dula's hand. Vinca looked worse than the rest of the people around the bed. Cerise and Sorrel were at the foot of the bed with looks that were seeping anger into the air around them, but otherwise seemed unbothered. The healers were tending to Dula's chest wound, which reminded Dula of the events leading up to this moment.

"How long was I asleep?" she asked the healers before squeezing Vinca's hand.

"Queen Dula, you've been unconscious for six days now," the healer said as she applied a brown paste to Dula's arm.

When Dula's face clouded with confusion, Cerise filled her in. "It was the wizards."

"They must have tried to steal your powers, Geena especially. When they failed, you went after Geena and the two of you fought, which landed you here," Sorrel related to Dula. "The other wizards must have taken Orrin and escaped. Their hut was torn apart and looked like someone had removed everything important from it, even the kitchen knives."

"The boy and Geena were in here the day before with some questionable injuries." The healer paused from applying and massaging the paste on Dula to speak. "Whatever they attempted did not go well for them."

"They took Orrin." Vinca's voice was raw and filled with emotion. "Do you think they'll hurt him?"

"They won't," Sorrel answered. "The half-breed wants family more than power. The rest of them I can't tell you what they want but they'll keep Orrin safe to keep the half-breed with them."

"Don't call Geena that!" Vinca snapped at Sorrel.

"SHE BETRAYED US!"

"We don't know that. We don't know what happened and shouldn't assume until we know more." Vinca's voice was quiet in comparison to Sorrel's booming outburst, but her voice never wavered.

"She betrayed us," Dula said as she focused on her hands in her lap, knowing that if they could look into her eyes, they would know it wasn't the truth.

"We'll find them and bring Orrin back home," Sorrel spoke, patting Dula's leg before walking out of the room, followed by the healer.

"First that insipid witch and now her spawn have caused so much turmoil in our home. When will the rest of you learn that wizards are nothing but bad news for us?" Cerise's voice was all venom. She stomped out of the room, almost like a pouting child.

The healer room fell silent, empty except for Dula and Vinca who had lived together for decades at this point, and knew each other better than they knew themselves. Dula knew that there was a chance Vinca would see through the lies, but hoped for her safety she at least wouldn't question it.

"Dula," Vinca began, "tell me the truth."

————

The van in front of them was old, the aged red paint was chipped and the doors were screaming in protest as Meda opened them to look inside. Geena and Orrin were the only ones who did not know how to drive but apparently most wizards use vehicles to get around, especially families with younger kids. Teleporting or any of that magic was hard to do with more than just yourself.

"Absolutely not." Pandora looked to the girls who found the van, rolling her eyes at the decision.

"Mom, we can use magic to make it look and run better. No one will know the difference," Meda insisted.

"I'll know." Pandora started to walk away before shouting over her shoulder, "I'll be back, give me half of an hour."

So they sat down and waited. Mirzam passed out some small snacks for them to eat. Geena changed the bandage on Percy's wound after cleaning up the dried blood around it. Whatever venom their sister had on the blade was still affecting his recovery, even after it had been removed from his system. His blood wasn't clotting well enough which meant that his bandages had to be changed more often than he liked, but he did not mind when Geena did it. Meda and Mirzam just ripped off the bandages and burned the germs off of his skin with a liquid that humans used.

While they were joking about how ugly the red van was, a vehicle quietly drove up and the window rolled down to reveal a smirking Pandora.

"What kind of car is this?" Geena asked.

"It's a Land Rover."

"Mirzam, how do you know that?" Geena asked.

"It says it on the car."

{ **19** }

CHAPTER NINETEEN:

The room was completely destroyed when Cepheus entered. The doors were barely on their hinges and there was a pile of mysterious parts. He recognized some vampire and werewolf parts, but he couldn't help the smile that crossed his face as he saw the golden eyed faerie—his head was the only part he allowed her to keep.

"Eris, you can't keep all of this for decor. Clean up," Cepheus spoke, interrupting his daughter as she threw knives at a picture of her siblings on the wall.

"They took Mother." Eris' voice was calm, which was never a good sign. "I will kill every single one of them, burn them and anyone they love, and turn the ashes into gems I will use as a crown."

"Darling, we will get your mother back."

"Do you even give a shit about her?" Eris stalked toward him, staring him down.

"Of course I do, but being emotional does not do anything except keep me from what I want. I've already spoken to our other faerie friends; Pandora is not in Apatite, but neither are any of the wizards that were staying there."

Eris looked at her father with blazing eyes peeking through her inky black hair. "Can I track them down my way or are you going to make me do this your way?"

Cepheus smiled and it reached his eyes which were glowing with excitement. "Darling, I do believe my way is more painful, but if it doesn't work I'll set you loose on the world."

Eris' chaotic demeanor calmed; only the promise of violence would soothe the fire in her soul. When Cepheus saw her eyes mellow out to a golden brown in place of the fiery orange, he knew she wouldn't be a risk anymore. While his first two failures were too small for his chains to fit, when Eris was under his control, she was perfect and couldn't even tell she was capable of life beyond his chains. He controlled her, she was his greatest weapon, ready to pounce on his command and only lived to please him. She was his perfect creation, perfect weapon.

"Pandora will be home soon and if we're lucky, I'll bring back two toys for you to play with."

————

Having a car made it easier for the group to keep moving even while some licked their wounds. Pandora, the least traumatized and injured of them, remained in the driver's seat for hours. The others sat in silence as soft music played through the speakers, ignoring Percy's request to be in charge of the radio. Pandora informed him that she could only tolerate so much of the human music he listened to before she would lose her cool exterior.

Mirzam was scribbling notes around a drawing of something cylindrically shaped. "What are you working on?" Geena asked, confused as the object appeared to be smoking on the page Mirzam was writing on. Carefully, she leaned in closer to further inspect it.

"Let me show you," Mirzam waved her wand over the page and it materialized in front of them the same way the blueprints did, placed still in Mirzam's lap. "This is the tool I have developed to disable our magic or any sort of power temporarily." Mirzam rotated so Geena could see all of it. "I need to work on it because it didn't last as long as it was supposed to when we went to go save you. Orrin or

Dula's powers kicked in sooner than they should've." Mirzam looked at Geena and shrugged. "I'll tweak it."

"I don't know how and I'm not strong enough to try and show you but that was me, actually." Geena felt everyone's eyes on her, even Pandora's brief glance through the rearview mirror. "The water was me. Not even Dula or my dad were able to use their powers yet."

"I'll add that to the list of things about you that intrigue me," Mirzam stated before returning her figure to her paper and continuing to scribble notes.

"She's interested—well actually, we are all interested in how you manage successful and controlled magic without a wand," Meda said, nudging Geena with her elbow. "You'll teach us when we find a place to stay for a bit, yeah?"

"Of course."

The voice was small but no one missed it from the second back row of the vehicle. "Are we going to be okay?"

Geena turned to see Percy cradling his injured arm with a look of uncertainty that made her heart clench. Geena held her hand out to him over the seat and smiled when he took it. She didn't know if they all would be okay, but that moment was all it took for her to promise that she would do anything, everything in her power to make sure Percy was okay.

"You'll be fixing us pancakes soon enough Percy," Geena told him with a smile and when he smiled back she could see that his moment of vulnerability was fading, and she turned back to face forward in her seat. The car was quiet for a while after that as they headed south toward the Hematite faerie clan. The sun was bright and a warm red as it tucked itself behind the trees in the distance. Geena was thinking of some of the places she stayed with her mom when they were on the run, when their silence was interrupted.

"Hey guys, I think I got blood on the seats."

"That's why I made sure to get a car with leather interior," Pandora spoke over Percy continued mumbles and winked when Geena met her eyes in the rearview mirror.

———

"You'll be careful, yeah?" Geena asked Orrin as the others set up a tent between some trees.

"I will. I'll come back with either good news that we have a place to stay for a few days or good-ish news that we get to continue our road trip." Orrin answered her, tucking some of her hair behind her ear as it was being caught in the wind and would get in her face.

"Road trip?"

"I'm trying out being optimistic. I don't quite like it."

Orrin was going alone to the Hematite clan to advocate on their behalf, and they would stay behind until they heard from him. Despite having to tell Orrin goodbye for a bit, Geena laughed. It didn't alleviate all of the stress but it let her enjoy this moment with her dad, Orrin. She was finding it easier to refer to him as her dad.

"Stay close to the rest, but not too close to the mother. I can't figure her out yet."

She nodded at him and went over everything, making sure he had all the supplies he needed to hold him over until he returned.

"Geena! Can you come clean Percy's shoulder, he keeps bitching when the rest of us try?" Meda was clearly exasperated.

"One second!" She lunged at Orrin, wrapping her arms around him and holding him so tight that she didn't think he could breathe, but Orrin held her just as tightly. "One day we'll be alright."

"One day," He agreed with a nod before planting a light kiss on her forehead. "I'll see you soon."

Lucia Jex-Blake is from rural North Carolina and has dreamed of being an author for most of her life. Artifacts of Fae is Lucia's first book. She is currently working on her bachelor's in English. In her free time, Lucia loves listening to a variety of music and watching more movies and TV shows than she has time for.